No one could throw a kiss into sexual overdrive like McBride.

Images of the two of them skin-to-skin, rediscovering each other's bodies, streaked through her mind. Though they were in a truck on the side of the road, she still wanted to strip away McBride's clothes. Worse, she wanted him to tear off hers.

All that pent-up desire was unleashed from a single mind-blowing kiss that got more potent the longer it went on. She should end it before her sanity dissolved. But his hands were cupping her face, the back of her neck, holding her in place so he could ravish—yes, actually ravish—every inch of her mouth. And she was loving it.

Instead of going with wisdom, she matched him stroke for delicious stroke with her tongue. There was a smoky darkness, an element of danger in the way he touched her. It hinted at some never quite spoken vice she'd been warned by her father not to want or accept. And never to enjoy.

The memory of that warning rang through her mind when it was displaced by another sound— two echoing gunshots, fired directly at them.

JENNA RYAN

DAKOTA MARSHAL

Harlequin®

TORONTO NEW YORK LONDON
AMSTERDAM PARIS SYDNEY HAMBURG
STOCKHOLM ATHENS TOKYO MILAN MADRID
PRAGUE WARSAW BUDAPEST AUCKLAND

To Kathy, who makes it all work.

Recycling programs
for this product may
not exist in your area.

ISBN-13: 978-0-373-69565-2

DAKOTA MARSHAL

Copyright © 2011 by Jacqueline Goff

ABOUT THE AUTHOR

Jenna started making up stories before she could read or write. Growing up, romance always had a strong appeal, but romantic suspense was the perfect fit. She tried out a number of different careers, including modeling, interior design and travel, but writing has always been her one true love. That and her longtime partner, Rod.

Inspired from book to book by her sister Kathy, she lives in a rural setting fifteen minutes from the city of Victoria, British Columbia. It's taken a lot of years, but she's finally slowed the frantic pace and adopted a West Coast mindset. Stay active, stay healthy, keep it simple. Enjoy the ride, enjoy the read. All of that works for her, but what she continues to enjoy most is writing stories she loves. She also loves reader feedback. Email her at jacquigoff@shaw.ca or visit Jenna Ryan on Facebook.

Books by Jenna Ryan

HARLEQUIN INTRIGUE

CAST OF CHARACTERS

Alessandra Norris—The Rapid City veterinarian's life is peaceful, until her ex comes crashing back into it.

Gabriel McBride—As a U.S. marshal, he is accustomed to danger, but when a hit man's bullet catches him off guard, the only person he can turn to is Alessandra.

Rory Simms—The escaped felon is unpredictable, desperate and deadly.

Casey Simms—The head of a powerful criminal family, she hired a hit man to take out McBride. But what else has she done?

Eddie Rickard—Alessandra saw the hit man on McBride's tail. Now she's a target, too.

Larry Dent—This small-town man wants to help, but can he be trusted?

Raven—The woman knows how to fight, but is she friend or foe?

Mystery Shooter—More than one person is out to get Alessandra and McBride.

Chapter One

The bullet that knocked U.S. marshal Gabriel McBride into the giant boulder caught him just below the left shoulder. Close enough to his heart to be a problem—if he'd actually believed he had a heart. He felt the blood and—hell, yes—the pain, but no way was he going to fold up and die because some low-life hit man had gotten lucky.

He estimated the distance from the boulder to the road, waited until the next spectacular fork of lightning faded, then, using the darkness as a cover, ran for his truck.

Once inside, he drew a deep, grimacing breath and checked the wound. His jacket and shirt were soaked. With blood as much as rain, he suspected. Which rendered his next decision moot. He was approximately ten miles from Rapid City, South Dakota, shot and disinclined to call the people he should for help. That only left one option. Alessandra.

Fighting pain that speared white-hot through his arm and torso, he got the engine started. In spite of everything, a faint smile flitted across his lips. Alessandra would either cure him or kill him. Only she and God knew which way it would go.

Maybe he knew, too, but his thoughts were begin-

ning to haze, so when he pictured his beyond beautiful veterinarian ex holding a scalpel, she wasn't necessarily using it to dig a bullet from his body.

Swinging the truck off the road one-handed, McBride relied on his memory rather than the headlights to guide him through the murk. A vivid flash of lightning had him swearing and pivoting left. He'd almost slammed into one of the rocks that lined the mountain road.

Concentrate, he told himself, and not on scalpels or death. It was three miles to the highway, another six to Alessandra's door. With luck, he'd spot his quarry on the way and find the strength to haul him in. Without it, big sister's hit man would cut him off and finish the job he'd started.

Swiping his good forearm over his face, McBride let both hit man and quarry go, fought the dizziness that wanted to sweep in and consume him and focused on Alessandra.

If tonight was his last night on earth, he wanted to die with her in his head. As she had been since he'd wedged aside a mangled piece of metal on a crumpled northbound bus and encountered her stunning gold eyes.

"YOU COULD DO worse, much worse, than date my nephew." Alessandra Norris's assistant, Joan, tapped the veterinary clinic's laptop. "By the way, how do you spell the dog's last name?"

On her knees, Alessandra smiled. "You're joking." She gave the black-and-tan German shepherd a quick scratch behind the ears before palpating his kidneys. "You can spell Phoenix, but not Smith?"

"It's been a long day." Joan's blue eyes rose to the fluttering overhead light. "Storm's getting worse, and this pooch is as healthy as Rin Tin Tin in his prime. Why was his owner so insistent we check him out tonight?"

"Because he just bought the dog, and the two of them are heading south tomorrow."

"Not in that rattly old truck they rolled up in, they're not."

"The truck's borrowed. They're going by bus."

Her assistant's eyebrows rose. "He's taking a dog on a bus?"

"Hey, I didn't make the plans."

"You don't ride buses, either." Joan gave her a look. "My sister and I are taking our usual tour bus trip to Las Vegas this fall. It's fun. You'd meet lots of interesting people. That's people, Alessandra, not dogs. Every year we encourage you to come, and every year you say no." She shook an accusing finger. "When you've got a phobia, you should march right up and spit in its eye."

Alessandra listened to the dog's heart. "Beat's good." Then she removed her stethoscope and scratched the animal's chin. "I almost got killed riding a bus, Joan. You know that."

"But you didn't, and in the end, you wound up meeting your husband."

"Soon to be ex-husband."

"We'll see."

Standing, Alessandra stretched out her lower back muscles. "Is there some reason we're having this conversation at ten o'clock at night, in the middle of a storm that's going to knock the power out and probably screw up half of tomorrow's appointments?"

"Tomorrow's Saturday. You're off. Doc Lang'll be stuck with any post-storm problems. Now, I want a commitment. Either you agree to come to Las Vegas with me and Lottie, or, come September, you get yourself ready to meet my nephew. McBride'll sign those divorce papers eventually. When he does, you'll be footloose and fancy free." Alessandra's sixty-year-old assistant slitted a shrewd eye. "That's what you want, isn't it? To be done with what was so you can move on to what will be?"

Alessandra hooked the lead onto Phoenix's collar. The dog had a flecked white mark in the shape of an arrow on his back. Her childhood dog, a brown lab, had had a mushroom-shaped mark that ran from its ears to the— Whoa! Where on earth had that memory come from? she wondered. Unless it was part of a much bigger memory involving a bus trip gone bad, a childhood home left behind and a future ex.

Shaking it off, she patted the German shepherd's butt. "Are you this pushy with Dr. Lang?"

"I'll be worse than pushy if he leaves his wife of fifty years."

"McBride and I were together for less than a tenth of that time."

"Your math's off, Alessandra. You and McBride met seven years ago, back when he was a cop."

"And the memories keep on coming." Opening the door to the reception area, Alessandra raised her voice above the thunder outside. "Phoenix is in great shape, Mr. Smith."

The dog's owner, a beanpole with hollow cheeks and awkward hands, stood immediately. "Thanks again for seeing us, Doc. I hope you won't have any trouble getting home in the storm."

"I grew up in Indiana. This is just a summer shower. Good luck in the Southwest."

Leaving him to settle the bill with Joan, Alessandra returned to the examining room.

Gusting wind drove the rain in sheets against the

windows and walls. Not a fit night for man or beast, she thought. Then she busied herself with anything and everything that would help stop her mind from drifting back seven years. Not enough, unfortunately. McBride's face had a way of sneaking in even when her guard was up. But tonight Joan hadn't merely damaged that guard; in typical jackhammer fashion, she'd punched right through it.

Smith and his dog were rattling off when she closed the lab door and returned to the reception room. "Go home, Joan." She held up a computer disk. "I need to look at some back files before I leave."

Joan shed her pink smock. "Workaholism's the first sign, you know."

"Of what?"

"Boredom, depression, withdrawal, take your pick. Make up or break up, I say." She fluffed her short platinum curls. "Personally, if I'd nabbed myself a looker like McBride, I'd have stuck."

"Your ex-husband drove a big rig. Mine's a cop turned U.S. marshal. Believe me when I tell you there's a difference."

"And there we end it." Tugging on her rain gear, Joan pointed at the ceiling. "Those lights are hanging on by their fingernails. You'd best work fast."

She intended to, Alessandra thought when a buckshot blast of wind and rain blew in with her assistant's departure. One mile away, in the rancher she'd scrimped and saved to purchase, was a claw-foot tub, a bottle of wine and a retrospective movie, all with her name on them.

Sliding the disk into her computer, she wondered if it was a sad comment on the state of her life that the highlight of a mid-August Friday night involved bubbles, pinot grigio and Cary Grant. Joan would say yes, but then Joan hadn't lived in the crazed nightmare that was Gabriel McBride's cop-dominated world for four-plus complicated years.

A rumbling peal of thunder shook the floor and walls. The lights and Alessandra's computer screen flickered. She poured a cup of coffee, eyed the ceiling, then turned her attention to the subject of bovine anatomy.

She hadn't done anything wrong, she was sure of it. The calf that had lost its life to a massive infection had been, essentially if not literally, dead before the breeder had called her.

Unless she'd missed something...

The breeder, furious and threatening, insisted she had. What could an outsider possibly know about prize bulls?

By "outsider" he meant "female." But it didn't matter to her, since the breeder's opinion of Dr. Stuart Lang, who'd been practicing medicine in South Dakota for the past forty years, was equally low. Glancing at scanned copies of the letters she'd received from the breeder shortly after the calf's death, Alessandra sighed. If words could kill, she'd be dead several times over by now.

Thirty minutes later, with the lights flickering and rain still lashing the windows, she closed the file and rocked her head from side to side.

Phone threats, written threats, Joan's threat—blind date or bus trip—a dead calf and a feeling of guilt that wouldn't subside... All in all, she'd had better weeks. Which made her plans for that night even more appealing.

She needed moments of solitude, sometimes craved them. Her father, a staunch Mennonite farmer, hadn't understood why. Neither had he understood or approved of her desire to leave the comfort of a close-knit community and board a bus for Chicago. What could college there offer her but headaches and problems? Better to stay in Holcombe, Indiana, marry the boy next door and turn two small farms into one.

She'd looked at Toby next door, then at the application in her hand. Not that Toby wasn't sweet, but Northwestern had easily outpaced him. She'd wanted to save animals, not farm them.

She'd also wanted—and gotten—an adventure.

A bus ride gone bad had bled into a hero's rescue, a marriage, a separation, a chance meeting with an aging vet and, finally, a pending lawsuit.

Taking a last sip of coffee, Alessandra wondered how Toby and the farm thing would have worked out. She'd probably be hiding chickens from her hubby's ax. Better the lawsuit, she decided.

The smoke detectors gave a long screech and a second later the lights died.

The clinic had an emergency generator, but since there were no animals in residence and Alessandra knew the layout well enough to locate her purse and trench coat, she didn't bother starting it up. Instead, she collected her things and let herself out the back door.

Wind snatched at her hair and coat like claws. Her car would start, it would. Although she probably shouldn't have let a seventeen-year-old delivery boy tune it up as payment for a full sheet of lab work on his aging retriever.

Dr. Lang called her a soft touch. Joan used a less flattering term, but one look into the dog's big brown eyes and Alessandra had caved.

Since an umbrella was pointless, she made her way

across the pitted parking lot. She'd almost reached her car when a hand clamped onto her arm and swung her around in a rough half circle.

A fork of lightning illuminated the surly face of the calf breeder. He was big, bald and built like a bulldog. His eyes were flinty and he had no neck. The fingers that dug into her skin like talons tightened when she tried to shake him off.

Fear tickled her throat. Swallowing it, she met his glare. "Let go, Hawley."

"You set the law on me."

"I talked to the sheriff."

Lightning flashed again. His lips thinned. "You told him I threatened you."

"You did."

"I called you up, told you you'd pay for what you'd done. And, by God, you will." He took a menacing step closer, sank his fingers in deeper. "You don't know squat about farm animals. Hell, you couldn't wrestle a colt from its mama's belly if your life depended on it."

She wouldn't back down, would not give him the satisfaction of reacting to the vicious gleam in his eyes. "I think I could probably do a lot of things under those circumstances."

His scowl became a sneer, and he yanked her toward him.

"You talk a good game, Dr. Norris, but deep down I reckon you're really a spineless little city girl who should have stayed in Chicago." Another jerk, another fruitless attempt to free herself. Fear didn't so much tickle now as grip her insides.

He bared his teeth in a leer. "Maybe I can think of a fair payment, after all."

She caught the whisper of movement in her peripheral

vision while she was lining up a determined left to his barely visible Adam's apple. A hand descended on her shoulder, and a voice emerged from the darkness next to her.

"I think that's enough manhandling for one night, pal."

Shock kept Alessandra's fist balled as she snapped her head around to regard the profile of none other than Gabriel McBride.

His expression remained amiable, but the hand that reached out to yank the breeder's startled fingers away did so with no small amount of force.

Alessandra felt rather than saw Frank Hawley's sputtering outrage.

"Who the hell are you?"

"Who's not important. What is…" McBride's slight movement had the breeder sliding his eyes downward. Lightning illuminated both the Glock and the badge at the waistband of McBride's jeans.

"You're a cop?"

"Close enough to haul you in for attempting to harm the lady beside me."

"That lady's a killer," Hawley spat.

"Makes two of us. You've got five seconds to disappear. On six, you're coming with me."

Hawley showed his teeth again, this time in a snarl. He raised a finger, started to jab it, then curled it back and swung away.

McBride watched and waited through the next thunderbolt before asking, "What the hell did you do to the guy, Alessandra?"

She pushed his arm away. "Nothing. Let go of me."

"You're welcome."

Sighing, she sidestepped him. "Thank you. Now, will you please tell me what you're doing in South Dakota?"

The smallest of smiles touched his mouth. "Got a bit of a problem, darlin'."

He took one step back and, before she could reach for him, dropped like a stone to the rain-soaked ground.

Chapter Two

"No hospitals, Alessandra. No cops. Say it."

McBride was hanging on to consciousness by a fine thread. Experience told Alessandra that thread wouldn't be allowed to snap until she made the required promise.

He held and shook her wrist. "I need you to say it."

There was no decision, really. If she didn't agree, he wouldn't let her help him. If she didn't help him, he'd die.

"Yes, all right, no cops."

"Or hospitals."

"I heard you, McBride." She attempted to lever him up. "I can't carry you, though. You'll have to help me."

Alessandra used all her strength to get him to his feet and into the clinic—and all her will not to go against her word. He'd been a cop once. Now he was hiding from them. Every shred of common sense she possessed told her to do what was necessary, then walk away. She also knew she wouldn't listen to it. She never did.

And so the nightmare would begin.

HE DIDN'T KNOW where he was because everything had gone black and weird. He felt like he was being dragged over a wet, rocky mountain. Water splashed onto his face, and the whole left side of his body felt numb. Until he took a wrong turn and ran straight into a red-hot knife.

He heard Alessandra's voice. It sounded far away. She wanted him to help her.

Help her with what?

The darkness was split by twin headlights on a twilight road.

The pavement was old, chewed up. The guardrail, where it existed, tilted into the canyon below.

He thought he was driving south, but direction didn't matter, because suddenly there was a sea of lights, red and flashing. He braked behind one of several ambulances.

A biker watched from the sidelines. "Bus went through the guardrail," he said, pointing. "Took the turn too sharp and started to roll."

Now McBride heard screams and saw people, wild-eyed and bleeding, as rescue workers assisted or carried them out of the canyon.

One of them, a man with a heavy accent, was hysterical. A woman sitting close to him had been impaled by a long piece of glass. He'd never seen anyone die before.

Lucky guy, McBride thought.

He identified himself to the officers on scene, then, without waiting to be asked, started down.

More people were being stretchered upward, among them the driver. They didn't know how many passengers might still be on board, but figured the bus wasn't going to remain much longer on the ledge where it had landed.

McBride agreed. The thing was rocking like a drunk ready to topple.

He skidded down the treacherous slope, spotted a firefighter spraying foam on the undercarriage so flying sparks wouldn't ignite the fuel tanks.

"There's at least two more inside," the man shouted. "I can't get them out and stop this sucker from blowing at the same time."

Nodding, McBride switched direction. He spied a man, facedown in a patch of scrub. Blood had pooled around his head. He wasn't breathing.

But somebody was. Fists pounded on one of the rear panels.

The only way in was through the front. He had to crawl over the impaled woman and, nearby, an older female who'd been crushed by a row of seats.

The pounding stopped. He muscled a chunk of twisted metal aside, was about to call out, when a woman's face appeared.

She was bruised, filthy and looked to be no more than eighteen years old. He noted both relief and suspicion in her eyes.

"I'm a cop," he said, because right then he knew he didn't look like one. "Detective McBride, Chicago P.D." The few lights still working illuminated the most amazing pair of gold eyes he'd ever seen. "Is there anyone else?"

"There was. Now there's only me."

He motioned for her to give him her hands. "We need to get out of here before the tanks blow or this bus goes for a second roll."

Once free of the wreck, he kept her ahead of him on the upward climb. She had a truly spectacular butt and mile-long legs to go with it. Her hair was dark, her features nothing short of extraordinary. She was headed for Chicago to become a vet.

Now how did he know that…?

A paramedic and a cop, both about to descend, met

them at the top. The paramedic took the woman aside. The cop, a friend, began strapping on gear.

"Figured it was you down there. Anyone left?"

McBride hoisted himself over the edge. "Not alive."

The cop continued to harness up. "It's a mess, all right. Like you. Why the beard and long hair?"

"Undercover case screwed up. I needed to get out of Chicago."

The woman hissed as the paramedic cleaned one of her cuts. "I guess I'm lucky your case didn't work out."

A smile crossed McBride's lips. Through a thickening haze, he bent to kiss her. "Maybe we're both lucky, Alessandra."

She grinned, though her features were cloudy now. "You're slipping, McBride. I didn't tell you my name..."

The memory skidded to a halt. Wait a minute. She hadn't said that. And he hadn't kissed her. Not there. Not then.

Oh, he'd kissed her all right and more, much more, but that was later, when he couldn't get her out of his head—and after he'd discovered she was twenty rather than eighteen.

Then his life had tanked and landed both of them in hell.

Pain sliced through him like a lightning bolt. It shattered all the images in his mind—the bus, the sobs, the screams, the sirens, everything. Except for Alessandra's eyes.

McBRIDE WAS, WITHOUT question, the most stubborn man Alessandra had ever met. Fortunately, he was also the most resilient. The moment she removed the bullet, which had come dangerously close to nicking a major artery, he'd fallen into a deep, healing sleep. She could almost see his red blood cells multiplying.

The generator outside growled noisily, but with the rainstorm disinclined to move on, she barely noticed it.

"Since when do you listen to Keith Urban?"

McBride's question came as no real surprise given his exceptional recuperative powers. But the clarity had her raising a brow as she emerged from the lab.

She had two scalpels in her hand and didn't put either of them down. "Joan left her iPod in the dock. I wanted music. How do you feel?"

"Like a man whose been shot, probed with a sharp instrument and left to die in a cowboy bar."

"So, well on the way to recovery, then." She held up one of the scalpels. "No double vision?"

"Not much vision at all." He squinted at the ceiling bulbs. "Is the power off?"

"It went out right before you arrived and subsequently fainted."

He half smiled. "I'll let that go, Alessandra, because I do, in fact, see two scalpels. I also heard your voice while I was floating around in the black fog of our distant past."

"Yes, you were reliving it fairly accurately until you got to the kissing part."

"Call it wishful thinking."

Alessandra looked at him and sobered. "Not that I want to be any more deeply involved than I am, but are you planning to tell me what you're doing here, minus a great deal of blood and with a hole in your chest where a bullet used to be?"

"Just another day on the job, darlin'." Wincing, he worked his way onto his right elbow.

She sighed. "You know you shouldn't do that, right?"

"I know a lot of things, Alessandra, some of them not particularly pleasant."

"Like the name of the person—possibly a cop, though I seriously hope not—who shot you? No hospitals, Mc-Bride? No police?"

"The shooter's name is Eddie. He's not a cop, but he is a pro, a dog with a bone, so to speak. And I'm the bone."

"So, nothing new in your world. Except that this time the bad guy did a little more damage than usual and is, in some twisted way, connected to the police."

He pushed up higher. "Your cynicism's showing."

"Removing bullets from people tends to bring it out." She struggled with mounting frustration. "Why is this Eddie after you? Or were you after him and somehow the scenario shifted?"

"The details aren't important. I'll explain the cop thing later. I was doing my job, Alessandra. I have no idea what you were doing with that no-neck jackass in the parking lot."

She could have told him it didn't matter, let him sleep for another few hours, then given him a prescription and suggested he return to Chicago to sort out his police-related problems. Her conscience would be clear, and the status quo would be restored.

However, whether or not he would have acted on it, Hawley had a mean streak, and he was as tough as the bull who'd sired the now-dead calf. McBride had gotten rid of him. That rated an explanation.

Setting both scalpels aside, she released her hair from its long ponytail and boosted herself onto a table. "Frank Hawley wants to make his fortune breeding bulls. He just doesn't want to spend a cent more than is necessary to keep them healthy. His farm's like a puppy mill for cattle. One of his calves got sick. He waited too long to call. The rest—well, you heard him. He thinks I'm a killer." Seeing him hoisting himself up, she hopped down and poked a firm finger into his chest. "The more you move, the more likely you are to reopen that wound."

"I know." Ignoring her warning, he swung his legs down and sat up, gripping the side of the cot. "What time is it?"

"It's 4:00 a.m."

"And the power's still out?"

"We're a little off the grid out here. Ergo, the big, noisy generator."

He moved a tentative shoulder, hissed in a soft breath and stood. "I have to get out of here."

"You realize that's suicide, right?"

"Give me some bandages, Alessandra, and whatever else you think I'll need to keep me on my feet. Then go home, and pretend none of this ever happened."

Irritation momentarily crowded out concern. "You never change, do you, McBride? You crash in, scare the hell out of me, tell me not to worry and then disappear."

He managed a weak smile. "That's why you left me. Which goes to show how smart you are. Or how stupid I am. One way or the other, you don't want to get mixed up in this."

Her answering smile had more of a bite, but she simply said, "I'll pack a medi-kit." Then she went into the back room.

He'd broken her heart once. She wasn't up for a repeat performance. Let some other female fall for his sexy, outlaw-cop charm. He was a good guy who read like a bad guy, and okay, yes, maybe he could still take her breath away with a look, but he didn't have to know that.

She wanted someone more stable next time, not a brooding, gray-eyed rebel who seldom had less than a three-day growth of stubble on his face, disliked the thought of scissors touching his hair and hated rules almost as much as he did the people who'd so carelessly brought him into the world.

Well, damn, she thought, exasperated, now she'd gone and dumped sympathy on top of righteous indignation. She really needed to speed his departure along.

She stuffed gauze, sterile tape and antibiotics that could be used on animals or humans into a makeshift medical pack, added rubbing alcohol, electrolyte water and iodine for good measure, then zipped it closed and swung the bag onto her shoulder.

Through the window she noticed a shadow pass by outside. Apparently McBride truly did want to be gone, and quick. She was more than happy to facilitate that desire. She opened the side door, intending to offer some comment in line with her mood, when a weak beam of light from the porch slanted across the shadow's face. It was not McBride.

Quickly she eased the door shut, not making a sound. Then she turned. "McBride!" She doubted he could hear her urgent whisper. Still holding the medi-pack, she ran for the lab. And plowed right into his chest.

He steadied her with his good hand as he glanced over her shoulder. "Is someone out there?"

"A guy with a gun. A big one."

"Did he see you?"

"I'm not sure. Maybe."

McBride stuffed the Glock he'd evidently retrieved into his waistband. "Can you describe him?"

"Long hair, ratty beard, nose ring." She let him nudge her to a less visible exit. "Eddie?"

"Yeah." He kept his eyes moving. "Bastard. I drove in ten different directions before coming here. I thought I'd lost him." With a glance out the window and another behind them, he positioned her next to the door. "Stay right here, Alessandra. Don't move."

He drew his gun, pointed it up. Alessandra's muscles knotted.

The moment McBride left, she went for the medicine cupboard, unlocked it and pulled out the .45 Dr. Lang kept there. She had to go through his desk for the bullets. Grabbing her purse, she doused the scattering of overhead lights, shoved everything into a backpack, then froze when she caught a faint creak of hinges behind her.

Instinct told her it wasn't McBride. Careful not to make any sound, she ran back to the door, took a quick look into the rain and slipped out onto the wraparound porch.

She saw McBride's black truck—barely—in a far corner of the lot. A light appeared, then vanished, in one of the examination rooms. Eddie must be working his way through the building. With an eye on the window, Alessandra inched carefully along the wall. "I'm going to kill you if Eddie doesn't," she whispered to the absent McBride.

She saw something a split second before a hand snaked around her neck and covered her mouth.

"Not a sound, sweet thing," a man's Southern-accented voice whispered in her ear. "I need to know where that slippery badass I shot and I reckon you helped has gotten to."

She should have loaded Dr. Lang's gun. That was Alessandra's first and pretty much only thought. Instead, a greaseball with bad aftershave had his gun pressed into her neck and was dragging her around the porch.

"Sorry to say, I'm gonna have to do you, but not until the badass is as dead as my cheating ex-wife." He inclined his head again, and she heard the grin in his voice. "I upped my rate when I heard McBride was the target. Come on now, you can tell old Eddie, how bad's he shot up? One to ten. Use your fingers."

She held up two, ordered herself to move with him, to keep breathing, to think.

"Is that all?" He sounded pissed off, but only for a moment. Then the grin returned. "Or could it be you're lying to buy time?"

Although his breath smelled of beer, he didn't sound drunk. He continued to haul her sideways. Alessandra waited, counted.

"C'mon, McBride," the hit man growled through his teeth. "I got the girl. Play hero, and…" The rest came out as a shocked curse.

He hadn't noticed the single step down to his right. Off balance, he let her go as he stumbled, then slammed into the clapboard wall.

Alessandra didn't hesitate. She scrambled from the porch.

"You come back here!" Still off balance, Eddie fired. Unsure if she'd been hit, Alessandra ran for the corner of the building.

She heard a thud. Two more shots whizzed past.

"Get to my truck," McBride shouted.

Looking back, the only thing Alessandra saw was a blur of rain and motion.

Another bullet discharged. Eddie swore again in a wheeze, and got off two more shots.

A hand gripped her arm. "Inside," McBride ordered.

He shoved her through the driver's side door. "Stay down."

She knelt on the floor in front of the passenger seat and tried to determine if either of them had been injured.

Once in the truck, McBride fishtailed out of the lot one-handed, his eyes on the rearview mirror. "Man, he's packing four semiautomatics."

Was that some sort of twisted admiration in his voice?

"How can you possibly—" She broke off when she glimpsed his shoulder. "You're bleeding."

"I know. He got me in my bad arm when I tackled him." He swung the truck down a narrow road.

Bracing for the potholes, Alessandra stole a brief look out the back window before climbing up into her seat. "You need to stop and let me restitch that wound."

"Not until we put some miles between us and Eddie."

"McBride, you can't ignore the laws of medicine forever. Lose enough blood, and you will die."

His eyes were still fixed more on the mirror rather than the road in front of them. "I'll do that a lot faster if we don't lose him."

Twisting around, Alessandra risked another glance, saw nothing and stared at his profile. "Who is that guy, and why does he want you dead?"

"Us dead," McBride corrected. "And I'm really sorry about that part."

"So am I." However, since she knew he meant it, she breathed through her irritation. "Talk to me, McBride. Who sent a hit man after you and why?"

"Long story short, I was dispatched to apprehend an escaped felon by the name of Rory Simms. Rory's sister is one of those crime lords the FBI would love to have under lock and tossed key, but unlike Rory, Casey's smart enough not to get caught standing over a corpse, holding a smoking gun. That's murder one. Rory's in for twenty-five minimum. But big sister was afraid he'd go a little crazy inside, say things he shouldn't about the family business, so she engineered an escape. Now Rory's on the run, I'm on his ass and big sister's hit man's on mine."

"And the no-cops, no-hospitals thing is just you not wanting to be removed from the case?"

He regarded her shrewd face. "Would you go with that if I said yes?"

"Not even if I was twelve years old and you looked like Captain Jack."

Which he kind of almost did, but that was absolutely not the point.

She looked again, did a double take. Were those headlights bouncing far in the distance? She turned around as the tires slammed through a series of ruts. "Do you know where you're going?"

McBride narrowly avoided a low tree branch. "At this moment, no. Overall, yes. Rory's heading south. That means we are, too." The apologetic tone returned. "I didn't plan for you to be involved in this, Alessandra, but you can identify Eddie, so you are. I'd love to call in, get information, request backup, but I can't. The last time I did—right before I got shot—I let my boss and only my boss know where I was heading. And yet Eddie, who'd been chasing me until that time, suddenly wound up ahead of me."

"You think someone in your home office leaked the information to him?"

"To him or Casey."

"Unless Rory called Casey or Eddie himself and told one or both of them where he'd be."

"That'd be the logical explanation," McBride agreed.

When he hitched his injured shoulder, she noticed the bloodstain was spreading. "Problem is, I have a strong feeling Rory's not following Casey's orders. Which could be another reason Eddie's been dispatched—to take little brother to a place where he and Casey can have a nice long chat."

"And you know all this because?"

He flashed her a quick smile. "That's classified information."

"Meaning, you have a source within Casey's organization."

"And you thought being a cop's wife had no benefits." His smile widened slightly. "My X source is a guy I've known since I was a rookie and he was a street dealer. Casey's screwed him over a few times, so he came to me with a deal. I've held up my end, now he's holding up his. X overheard part of Casey's conversation with Eddie. He knew the assignment to track Rory was mine. He called me."

"Honest to God, McBride, I feel almost ridiculously cloak and dagger right now. Okay, you're convinced there's a leak in your office, but every police department in every state doesn't report to the Chicago division of the U.S. marshals." Hesitating, she slid him a sideways look. "Do they?"

"They do if one of the deputy marshals goes down. Gunshot wounds have to be reported, Alessandra, by hospitals and police. That puts information on the computer, makes it accessible to anyone who cares to find it."

"Specifically, a turncoat marshal."

"For one. My gut tells me there's somebody on the take in the Chicago P.D., as well, probably in Homicide."

She kept a close eye on the spreading bloodstain. "You've got names in mind, haven't you?"

Although the smile that had been hovering on his lips grew a little, there was no humor in it. "Yeah, I've got names in mind. Doesn't do me any good here and now, but it will when Rory's back in prison and I'm back in Chicago."

She searched the heavily treed road behind them for anything resembling a tail. "This uncharacteristic optimism is a treat, McBride. If I hadn't just dodged flying bullets, I'd actually applaud it." Something glimmered, and she looked more closely out the rear window. "Those are definitely headlights."

McBride's gaze slid to the rearview mirror. "They definitely are." He gave her unfastened seat belt a flick. "Buckle up and hold tight, darlin'." His eyes glittered with anticipation as he geared down. "This ride's gonna get wild."

Chapter Three

Surreal was the best description Alessandra could come up with for the next sixty minutes of her life. Somewhere between where they'd been and where they wound up, the rain stopped, the clouds broke apart and shafts of light began to filter through the trees.

By the time her mind slowed enough for her to register her surroundings, they were well into the mountains near what had probably once been a logging camp.

The moment McBride halted, she slid from the truck. Thick stands of pine and spruce towered over them. The fallen trees, now moss covered and decayed, were more likely the remnants of a windstorm than a timber man's ax. She let her head fall back and, finally, some of her tension ebbed.

"Please tell me we lost that creep, because five more minutes of those ruts and my brain will be permanently scrambled." He didn't answer. Rubbing her backside, Alessandra turned. McBride was still in his seat with his head resting on the back. His eyes were closed. She climbed back into the cab to shake him. "McBride. Are you conscious?"

"Enough to tell you there's only a fifty-fifty chance we lost him." He spoke but didn't open his eyes or move.

"That's better than your odds of surviving if you don't let me restitch that gunshot wound."

"Nag, nag, nag."

Alessandra refused to be alarmed by his pallor. Leaning over, she opened his shirt. The bandage covering the gunshot wound was soaked through. "Out of the truck, McBride."

A half smile grazed his lips. "Forest floor works better for you, huh?"

Straddling him, she caught his hair and pulled until his eyes finally cracked open. "I see a lot of clouds in there, pal."

"Yeah, but what are you feeling?"

Part of her wanted to laugh. Only McBride would be thinking about sex under these conditions.

"Apparently your sick mind hasn't changed since the last time I saw you." She pushed the door open. "How can you be hard when you're bleeding to death?"

His eyes closed, but the vague smile remained. "From where I'm sitting, best answer I can give you is, 'Duh.'"

"Great. I'm on the run with a crazy man." He was going to black out, she just knew it. She hopped off. "Time to get down and dirty."

She supported him by his good arm as he tumbled from the cab. An old gray blanket from the back served as a cot. Once he'd dropped onto it, Alessandra rolled up her sleeves and reached for the medi-pack.

"No sign of Eddie?" he asked in a slur.

"No sign, no sound, no need." Partly because he deserved it, but mostly in an effort to startle him awake, she gave the rubber tubing in her hand a snap, smiled, then bent down until her lips grazed his ear. "Let the bloodbath begin."

McBride surfaced to shadows that were thick and air that was heavy with the prospect of yet another rainstorm. His limbs weighed fifty pounds apiece, and he swore someone was using a blunt ax on the back of his skull. Still, he managed to get his eyes open and make the connection between his brain and his vocal cords.

"Where am I?"

Alessandra didn't seem the least bit surprised by the sudden question. "You're propped up against a fallen tree in the Black Hills of South Dakota, and, by some miracle, still alive." Sitting cross-legged in front of him, she folded a bunch of strange-looking leaves into a cloth and tied a string around it.

"Why don't I trust that serene expression on your face?"

"Relax. If I wanted you dead, you'd have passed on before sunset." She gave the string a hard tug.

Alarm bells began to clang in his head. "What's that?"

"A medicinal poultice. We use them on horses after they've been gelded." The glitter deepened. "I say 'we,' but I really mean *I* use them. Dr. Lang believes in the more traditional forms of pain management, his favorites being those that are introduced rectally."

"You're enjoying this, aren't you?"

"Only for the past thirty seconds. Until then, I was calling you a bastard in every colorful way I could think of."

He used his good hand to push himself away from the trunk. "You're father'd be pissed."

"No, he'd just straighten his shoulders, look stoically upward and blame my mother for influencing me. Then he'd sag and blame himself for giving in to temptation once and marrying her. I'm a sort of by-product of his lust. I don't think he's ever quite figured out where I fit into his straightforward, methodical world."

It was a tragedy, to McBride's mind, that Alessandra's mother had died of an aortic aneurysm mere days after her only child's eleventh birthday. Sadder still was the fact that she'd apparently really loved Alessandra's father. Why else would any sane woman endure twelve years of marriage to a man who lived, worked and would ultimately die by an archaic set of rules that were more of his own making than those of the religious order to which he belonged?

Alessandra's grandmother, her father's own mother, called him a tight-ass. Not in those particular words, but that was the gist. She'd liked her son's beautiful Bahamian-born wife and had, McBride knew, run interference for her granddaughter up to and including his and Alessandra's wedding day—which was an entirely different memory.

As if she'd been following his thoughts, Alessandra's lips curved. "You can puzzle it out for the rest of your life but you'll never understand him." She threw McBride the poultice and stood in a single graceful motion. "Sun's set, you need rest and I want a shower. I'm also hungry. All I found in your truck were nacho chips, candy bars and some energy drinks."

"Never know when you'll need a quick buzz."

"Mmm, I found the whiskey bottle, too."

"Buzzes come in many forms, Alessandra. You're right, though, we need to get out of here." The pain had less of a rapier-sharp edge after he worked his way into a crouch. He tucked the poultice in his shirt pocket. "Can you drive a loaded 4x4?"

He knew she was watching him for signs of disorientation. He must have passed the test, because she began folding the blanket. "On good roads, yes. On a wilderness obstacle course, we'll find out."

He could go with that. "Do you know where we are?"

"More or less." She caught his arm when he stood and the rapier took a nasty swipe at him. "I don't suppose there's any chance you'd consider returning to Rapid City."

He slanted her a dark look that brought a fleeting smile to her lips.

"Figured as much. In that case... Can you walk?"

Like a man who'd taken several pulls from that whiskey bottle. And her touching him didn't make him any steadier. Her father's thoughts for her mother were Puritanical compared to the ones currently flying through McBride's head. He knew and vividly remembered every inch of her butt, her legs, her breasts and, God help him, her hands. She'd learned lightning fast how to drive him straight to the edge and over.

When the pain sheared through him again, he welcomed it. "Keys are in the ignition, Alessandra. If you're sure you've got your bearings, we need to head southwest."

"That's the direction Rory's taking, huh?"

Fat drops of rain began to fall from the bruised clouds above. "Rory's heading for a border." Although climbing into his truck was roughly equivalent to scaling Mount Rushmore during an ice storm, McBride persevered. "He's zigzagging, wants me to believe he's going to Canada, but my money's on Mexico."

She stopped pushing to peer around his arm. "Are you serious? You expect me to go to Mexico?"

"Did I mention I was sorry?"

"Did I mention I put some of Dr. Lang's suppositories in that medi-pack?"

He managed to chuckle rather than wince. "Give me a viable short-term destination, Alessandra."

She sent him a last biting stare, then swung on her heel to point. "Bodene's about fifty miles southwest of here. Spruce Creek's thirty, but in a slightly different direction. Joan's rustic Dead Lake cabin's our best bet. It's a twisty twenty-mile drive from this old camp."

"Sounds good," he said. "Secluded." Ghoulish, too, but hopefully not portentous.

Rain began to pelt the roof and windshield. In the driver's seat, Alessandra tied back her hair in a long ponytail. Now how in hell could something so simple strike him as so damn sexy?

Once again, she seemed to know what he was thinking. Her lips twitched when she shoved the truck in gear. "Eyes forward, McBride. We're off to Dead Lake, and Eddie's nowhere to be seen."

Which was, McBride reflected as he scanned the eerily silent clearing, the thing that concerned him most right now.

JOAN'S CABIN HAD a bathroom, a galley kitchen, a huge stone fireplace and a pull-out sofa that faced the hearth.

"Home sweet home." Alessandra dropped her gear on a small window table. "It's compact, but not all that different from my father's house. There's even a loft." Humor invaded her tone. "No ladder."

Overhead lights flared at the touch of a switch, as did the propane water heater.

"Quick trip into town for supplies, and I can have my long-awaited shower."

McBride, who'd recovered even more rapidly than she'd anticipated, made a more purposeful circle of the room.

"There's a lot of glass," he noted. "And trees for cover."

"There's also a good chance we left Eddie in one of those potholes we slammed through last night." She halted him by setting her palm on his chest. "The rain's stopped, there's a general store just over a mile from here and, honestly, given a choice at this moment, I'd rather die from a bullet than from starvation. We've seen, you've scoped, let's go."

"You'd make a lousy marshal, Alessandra."

"I'll take that as a compliment." But she waited while he checked out the porch and small yard before returning to his truck.

"I'll drive," McBride told her. "Put on my leather jacket and hat, and try not to let anyone in town see your face. We go in and out, no hesitation. Basics only."

Alessandra tipped back the brim of the hat he'd dropped on her head and frowned. "Have you been spending time with my father?"

"Better yours than mine. Which way?"

She indicated a narrow mud and gravel road. At his raised brow, she smiled. "I came here with Joan in June."

"Did you go into the store?"

"Several times. The owner can't see anything clearly that's more than a foot in front of him." She gauged his mood, then went for it. "How's your father doing these days?"

He shrugged. "In jail, out of jail. Last I heard, he was being held in Panama. Something about flying an illegal substance across the border inside a shipment of Colombian coffee beans."

Alessandra thought back. McBride's dad had brought his fourth wife to their wedding. After the ceremony, he'd made a pass at her Bahamian aunt. As with most things, it hadn't worked out for him. Angelica had given him a resounding slap while wife number four poured a drink over his head. And all of that before the photographs had been taken.

"Maybe time in a Panamanian jail will straighten him out," she mused aloud.

"If you think that, you've been living in the animal world too long." McBride indicated a weather-worn structure. "Is that the store?"

"That's it. Dead Lake Feed, Seed and General Wares."

"There's only one vehicle out front."

"The year-round population here is about fifteen. The in-out thing should be relatively simple."

There was no one behind the counter when the cowbell jangled to announce their entry. Flies buzzed against torn window screens, and the refrigeration units, relics from the 1960s, made a loud humming noise.

Tugging McBride's hat lower to cover her face, Alessandra picked up two large baskets and headed for the grocery section. She filled up, then picked out some personal stuff.

Her arms were already straining when she turned a corner and spied the clothes and underwear. Although her choices were limited, pretty much everything she needed was available. Except that she had to climb up to the top shelf to dig out the right sizes. She even snagged a pair of suede hiking boots and a sleeping bag.

On her way to the cash counter she found McBride with his hip perched on a dusty windowsill as he scanned the deserted road outside.

He turned his head, saw the overflowing baskets and grinned. "That's your idea of in and out?"

"Why, yes, thank you, I'd love some help." She

handed him the heavier basket and shook her arm to get the circulation back. "Is there a cashier?"

"Not that I've seen. I could have loaded a pickup with stolen merchandise by now."

"Mr. Singer?" She tapped the service bell. "You have customers."

When no one approached, Alessandra peered over the counter to her left. And spotted a pair of feet.

"Damn. McBride!" Without waiting, she flipped up the pass-through.

The elderly storeowner lay facedown on the floor. She was searching for a pulse when the stockroom door burst open.

Alessandra glimpsed torn jeans and heard a snarling curse. Then her eyes snapped up, and she saw the gun.

ACTUALLY, IT WAS a rifle, and the thief nearly dropped it in his rush to escape.

Packs of cigarettes spilled from the inside of his zipped jacket. He hurdled Alessandra and the store owner, scrambled under the pass-through and took a swing at McBride.

She would have jumped up, but the owner's bony fingers snared her wrist and held fast.

"Boy got hold of some funny mushrooms," he whispered hoarsely. "His ma called me right before he barged in. She reckons he's seeing pink elephants about now."

Hearing a thwack, Alessandra raised her head. No surprise, the thief hadn't gotten past McBride. "Don't think so. Stars, maybe." She returned her attention to the fallen man. "Are you hurt?"

"Winded." With her help, he got slowly to his feet. "Thought it best to take a dive when the boy barreled in and knocked me aside... Oh, there we go, neat as you please." He beamed at McBride, who was crouched next to the dazed youth. "Now, you put those smokes back where they belong, young man. I'll take the rifle," he said to McBride, who was currently holding it. "It's just a BB, but that's plenty dangerous when your bones are as brittle as mine." Repositioning his glasses, he hobbled over to the counter. "These your baskets?"

The man's store-bought smile widened when he realized how much merchandise he was looking at. "Seems this is my lucky night, after all." He squinted at Alessandra. "You and your man fixing to camp a spell?"

"Yes—I mean, no." She glanced at McBride but couldn't read his expression in the dusky light. "Yes, we're going to camp. But not here." Inspiration struck. "We're on our way to Canada."

The old man sighed his disappointment. After he'd totaled the items, she understood why. "Nothing on special this week, huh?"

"Got a good price on hip waders."

"We'll pass." McBride handed over the necessary cash.

"Stick to portabello mushrooms," Alessandra advised the youth, who was slumped in a chair by the door waiting for his mother to arrive.

McBride practically airlifted her through the door and into his truck.

"I have a feeling you're not happy."

"Two people can identify us, Alessandra. That wasn't the scenario I was going for."

They bounced through a large dip and back onto the road. "Relax, McBride. The old man couldn't begin to describe us, and all that kid saw was two— Damn." She hissed out a frustrated breath. "I called you McBride back there, didn't I?"

"That you did, darlin'."

A 4x4 pulled out of a hidden road ahead of them. The driver wove from side to side for half a mile before finally veering into the parking lot of a ramshackle bar and grill.

"Wanna risk it?" McBride surprised her by asking.

She suspected he knew how she'd respond. "All those rusted-out pickups in the lot make the place look very Eddielike. Still, if he did follow us, maybe we'll get lucky, and he'll stop in, drink himself under the table and never make it to the general store."

"Always a possibility."

Out of nowhere, an indescribable sensation swept over her skin, as if a cold breeze had just passed over her grave.

Puzzled, she looked back toward the bar. No one was in the vicinity, only the rusty pickups and a tired-looking motorcycle. So why did she suddenly feel as if some evil entity was tracking their every move?

Chapter Four

One hot shower, one makeshift meal and one weird feeling later, Alessandra found herself pacing the cabin's interior like a caged tiger. Time alone to think wasn't necessarily a good thing, and she'd thought a lot in the five minutes it had taken McBride to shower.

He hadn't shaved, though, she noticed when he emerged bare-chested and with his jeans only half-fastened.

"What?" Her unintentional stare had him looking down at himself. "Did I forget something?

No, but she needed to. It shouldn't be legal for a man to be so sexy. Since she shouldn't be thinking that way, she drew a deep breath and resumed her pacing. "You're not bleeding."

A smile played on his mouth. "You make that sound like a bad thing."

"You should wear a bandage."

Towel in hand, he held his arms out to the sides. "Say the word, Alessandra. I'll even let you slip your poultice under the gauze just to show how much I trust you."

Drumming up her own smile, she met his eyes. "You're very brave, given the circumstances."

"And your deteriorating mood," he added.

"More like strained. It's only been one day and, to this point, our separation's been fairly amicable."

He moved closer, his gaze fixed on hers with a smoky intensity that would have unnerved her if she hadn't been prepared for the sexual punch.

"You won't get around me with smoldering looks, McBride. After four years of marriage and eighteen months apart, I've developed an immunity."

"You make me sound like measles."

"You're a different kind of danger, but still not something I need in my life right now."

He continued his unswerving advance. "What is it you want, Alessandra?"

She opted to take the loaded question at face value. "To go home."

"That's not possible. What else?"

"Stability."

"If you wanted that, you'd have stayed in Indiana and married the boy next door."

He was getting very close. Wisdom dictated she move away. She didn't.

"Trying to skew my thoughts won't work, either, McBride."

Another faint smile appeared. "It's not your thoughts I want to skew."

Okay, this was getting out of hand. She had every right to be annoyed at him for sucking her into the crazed vortex of his life. Her friends and his insisted he had a death wish, and while Alessandra didn't disagree, she saw it more as a burning need to prove that he was the antithesis of his father. Wherever the truth resided, however, now wasn't the time to delve into it.

Hooking a wistful finger in the chain around her neck, she toyed with the delicate links. "You didn't have to change your lifestyle or your goals for me. I told you that before we separated. I'm not a cop or a U.S. marshal, though I do applaud both professions. I used the wrong word when I said I was looking for stability. What I should have said was 'sanity.' You know the deal, McBride, a halfway normal life where I'd be met at the door after work by my pet, not by a homicidal junkie who's been hiding out behind our trash cans for the better part of the day, looking for a way to extract his revenge on the person who offered his girlfriend a deal in exchange for information."

"That was one incident."

"What about the guy who jumped out at us in a restaurant parking lot? Or the nut case who called our home and told me not to try starting my car? What about the candies that arrived courtesy of a drug lord you'd helped to expose?"

"There was nothing but candies in that box."

"It was the gift giver not the gift that was the point. For the first three years of our marriage you were undercover more than you weren't. And nothing got better when you ditched your badge and joined the U.S. marshals."

"You knew what you were getting into."

"Not as well as I knew what I was getting out of."

Averting his gaze from hers at last, he regarded the darkened window. "Your point." When he looked at her again, still at dangerously close range, she saw genuine regret in his features. "I never meant to involve you in this. Rapid City's where I happened to be when I got hit, and you were the only person I knew I could trust."

Okay, that wasn't fair. Before it could fully ignite, the spark fueling her temper fizzled and died, leaving in its wake a jumble of feelings she couldn't begin to separate.

"You always were good—" She halted as his gaze traveled past her and suspicion replaced regret in his features.

She turned but saw nothing in the misshapen shadows beyond the glass. "Is someone there?"

"Probably not. Get the lights just in case."

It wasn't exactly a reassuring remark. But she went for the switch and plunged the cabin into darkness.

"Now what?" she asked twenty silent seconds later.

"Shh."

He eased them both away from the window. Woodsy night sounds filtered in. Beyond that, everything had gone still and quiet.

Then a twig snapped in the nearby trees, and Alessandra's senses went on high alert.

Swearing softly, McBride reached for his gun in the back of his waistband.

One of the boards on the porch creaked. There was a rush of movement, a thud of feet and finally a crash as a rock flew through the front window. A split second later, the door slammed open. Emitting an attack cry, a man charged in, hands raised and clutching a very large ax.

EDDIE NOTICED the broken window first, then the tire tracks in the mud. Coming, going, maybe coming again. There was no truck in the vicinity, and no sign of movement inside.

It wasn't quite dawn. The sky was lightening but the shadows would hide him for another twenty minutes. Plenty of time to get the deed done.

He was savoring the moment when a light went on.

The front door opened and a man stumbled out. He was tall and dark haired, but too gangly to be McBride.

The fury that rose was swiftly expelled. Eddie looked at his vehicle, then back at the stranger currently doing his business off the side porch.

A half-naked woman emerged, wobbled in one direction, then the other, until she finally collided with the man. They giggled and staggered back inside.

The light winked out.

Should he do them, anyway, just for being in this remote cabin at this time when he'd been looking for McBride and the pretty veterinarian?

A nasty grin split his face. No. Leaving a trail of corpses was never a good thing. But he had extra guns, and as long as they were too drunk to walk straight, he might as well have a little fun. He'd cover his face with a bandanna, his head with a hat and do the stick-'em-up thing from behind.

If they had any information at all, they'd talk. Then depending on his mood, the inclination of his trigger fingers and whether or not they did something stupid, they'd either live or they'd die.

As for McBride and the pretty vet? Eyes on the prize, Eddie-boy. Bang, bang, cha-ching.

It amazed Alessandra that anything could shock her. However, a second wild-eyed, weapon-wielding youth in one night was too extreme even for McBride's world.

The young man, trailed by a girl in Daisy Dukes and flip-flops, blasted across the threshold with a Tarzan yell and more fear than aggression in his eyes. McBride disarmed him easily, knocking the ax from his sweaty hands and pinning him to the wall. Alessandra shook off her momentary trance and intercepted the girl as she made a beeline for McBride's back.

It took fifteen noisy minutes to sort through the confusion. Apparently the college-aged youth was Joan's nephew. He had his aunt's permission to use the cabin during his cross-state camping trip. Unfortunately for all of them, tonight was the night he and his girlfriend had reached Dead Lake.

Alessandra knew that she and McBride could have stayed in the cabin until morning. She also knew they'd be endangering innocent lives if they did. So they left. And drove for more than three hours before McBride agreed to stop.

Having been raised on a farm, Alessandra didn't consider herself a wilderness wimp. But sleeping in McBride's truck, then attempting to eat breakfast while swarms of mosquitoes, horse and deerflies did the same, proved next to impossible.

Deet was the only answer, and Alessandra wanted the sticky repellant gone as soon as possible. That meant another shower, this one in a crappy public facility that boasted slime-coated floors and a weak spray of barely warm water. They didn't get back on the road until midmorning.

More correctly, on the back roads. It was one wooded cow path after another, roughly stitched together.

"You know," she remarked with a quick hiss of pain for her abused backside, "unless he's taking this same route, which is unlikely for an escaped felon, Rory Simms will be in Mexico before we get out of the Black Hills."

McBride maneuvered around a two-foot gouge. "Rory's a slow mover, Alessandra. He's an even slower thinker. He's also not good on his own, which is why I figure he's heading this way."

"Am I supposed to accept that as an explanation?"

"He's making his way to his contacts." McBride divided his attention between the road, his laptop and the on-board map. "People his sister might not know about."

"Okay, obvious next question, if she doesn't know about them, how do you?"

He didn't quite avoid a missing chunk of road and as a result almost bounced Alessandra out of her seat. "You should tighten that strap."

She sighed instead. "Answer the question, McBride."

"Rory likes hookers. Some hookers accept money for services other than sex. My source inside Casey Simms's organization got a line on Rory's favorite prostitute. He paid, she talked, we scored."

"You hope."

"Yeah, there's that. But from the text I got last night, X thinks that no matter where Rory appears to be going, he's really taking an indirect route toward one of his contacts. As far as our particular route is concerned, think Eddie and the more twists and turns, the better."

"At the risk of sounding repetitive, if Rory's using the interstate or even a semidecent highway, he'll be there and gone before we reach the next mountain pass."

"We'll see," McBride said.

Too bruised and tired to pursue it, Alessandra let the subject drop. Keep talking and she ran the risk of biting her tongue off.

Although her pride seldom allowed her to complain, neither the day nor the traveling conditions improved. They weren't going in anything resembling a straight line. By late afternoon, she figured they could be anywhere from the Big Horns to the Rocky Mountains.

Fanning her face slowly with a service station map, she finally asked, "Where are we, McBride?"

"About twenty miles from Ben's Creek. There's a good chance Rory will be there."

"And hopefully Eddie won't." She stopped fanning to cock her head. "Isn't Ben's Creek north of Rapid City?"

He smiled in profile. "Your point being?"

"What happened to 'we need to head southwest'? Never mind." She waved him off. "Message from your X-man, indirect routes, et cetera. My brain's running on empty at the moment. Are you sure about this source of yours?"

"Sure enough. I got an email update while you were texting your assistant about what we were doing at her cabin last night and why you won't be coming into work tomorrow."

She summoned a pleasant expression. "If I said I hate you, would you be kind and ditch me in Ben's Creek?"

"I'll take that to mean you want to stop. Next place we pass, I promise."

True to his word, ten minutes later he pulled off the ancient two-lane highway that was probably only used by logging trucks now and into a dusty roadside clearing, complete with a tippy wooden shack, two gas pumps and a rear yard full of abandoned vehicles.

Alessandra took one look, stuck his hat on her head and shoved the door open. "I hate you, McBride. This place better have a washroom."

To her relief, it had two. The man tearing a seat out of an ancient Oldsmobile took one look at her and stabbed a thumb at the shack. "Ellie's my wife. Buy one of her blackberry pies, and she'll let you use her private john."

Alessandra thanked him, bought two pies and was immediately ushered into Ellie's paying-customers-only washroom.

It smelled like pine cleaner and the toilet did flush—if she pulled really hard on the chain. The cold-water tap almost worked, as well. The mirror didn't. A haze over the glass gave her face a tintype-photo look that would have made her laugh if she hadn't glimpsed the remnants of an old bus through the window behind her. The thing had fallen on its side like a drunk elephant with its fire-blackened underside fully exposed.

For a motionless moment, Alessandra's throat muscles seized, so badly that she couldn't swallow. Voices swarmed in her head.

An elderly man: "I'm off to Chicago to visit my brother...."

A geek: "I'll have this textbook read by the time we hit the city limits...."

A wispy woman from Arizona: "Excuse me, do you suffer from motion sickness...?"

A young marine: "I'm getting married in three months...."

Words and faces overlapped. She felt the floor moving, the bus skidding, rolling. She heard glass shatter, metal shriek, murmurs turn to screams.

With a huge effort, Alessandra tore her eyes from the mirror. But not until she saw another face that drifted in. McBride.

Sexy, smoke-gray eyes stared at her. "Don't worry, I'm a cop. Give me your hand. I'll get you out of here...."

"You all right, dear?" A rusty female voice shattered the spell.

Alessandra jolted back to the present. She breathed

out, dried her hands and checked her reflection one last time. "I'm fine, thank you."

When she opened the door, Ellie offered a toothy, yellow smile. "I thought maybe you'd passed out from the heat. We don't get many customers here, us being so remote and all. When we do, I like to give them a special parting gift."

Letting her smile grow bigger, she produced a knife from the pocket of her apron.

Chapter Five

The knife was the second thing McBride saw when he turned the corner inside the shack. The first was the startled expression on Alessandra's face. He would have knocked the woman called Ellie through the paper-thin wall if Alessandra hadn't glanced up and given her head a shake.

"It's to cut the pies," she told him quickly, and recaptured the woman's attention with a smile. "Thank you, for the pies and the gift."

Fifteen minutes later, and on the road yet again, McBride asked her, "You weren't sure about that knife at first, were you?"

She examined the serrated blade. "No, and I put the blame for my mistrust squarely on your shoulders. I used to think people were basically nice and well meaning. Lately, I see everyone as a potential front for a hit man." A sparkle in her eyes softened her words. "You are such a badass, McBride."

"Had a chat with Eddie while he was holding you, huh?"

"Yes, and I relayed our entire conversation to you while you were bleeding all over that old logging camp. How's your shoulder?"

"Poultice is helping."

After she tucked the knife away, he felt her eyes slide in his direction. "Your way's not working, is it?"

Damn. She knew him too well. Now it was time to either jump out of the truck or irritate her into silence by pretending not to know what she meant. He did neither.

"The dangerous cases just come to me, Alessandra. I don't go looking for them."

"Yes, you do. The more the danger, the more you like it. Because even though you balk at a by-the-book approach, you always get the job done. You were never meant to be married, or anything more than superficially involved with a woman. We made a mistake, an incredibly hot one for a while, but our marriage was wrong from the start. Death is your shadow, McBride. Except that one day the roles will be reversed. Death will be real, and you'll be the shadow. I need you to sign the divorce papers."

His stomach clenched, but beyond that, he didn't react. Didn't want to think about Alessandra as part of his past. He knew it was unfair to her, and really, if he'd been asked, he wouldn't have been able to explain to anyone, least of all himself, why he rejected the thought of divorce so completely.

"McBride, look out!"

When she made a grab for the wheel, he swore. Directly in front of them, in the middle of the road, stood a white-tailed doe and two half-grown fawns. He swerved, hit the brakes and felt the truck begin to slide.

The back end struck something—not one of the deer, he hoped—fishtailed and slammed into a large spruce. Which was the only thing that kept them from falling into the creek bed some thirty feet below.

Several seconds passed before Alessandra released a

slow breath. "If it's any consolation, we missed the deer. Did we damage anything?"

"Only the outer edges of my pride."

Her eyes danced a little. "So nothing important, then."

"I'll let you know in a minute."

It didn't take half that time to determine that the rear axle was bent. Not undrivable, but the work needed would cost more than just money.

With Alessandra's help, McBride changed the flattened left tire and limped the truck the rest of the way to Ben's Creek.

One of the things he'd always appreciated—and, yes, loved—about Alessandra was that she never bitched or berated. She did what she could, what she had to and left the rest to him.

The unpaved road widened, the terrain began to open up and the woods thinned as they approached the valley town of Ben's Creek. Small houses dotted the landscape. He saw a kid with an iPod, train tracks bordered by weeds half as high as his truck and a small filling station with three men sitting in chairs beneath the overhang.

Alessandra regarded the unmoving trio. "Doesn't look terribly promising, does it?"

"It'd look a lot better if they saw you."

Unfastening her seat belt, she stretched her back muscles. "I figure it'll take the better part of a day to repair that axle, McBride. Given the fact that it's after eight now, getting dark and I have no intention of sleeping in your truck again, someone in this town is going to see me. Might as well be these guys."

She had the door open before he could get his teeth unclenched. How the hell had she gotten more bewitching since their separation? More to the point, how was he supposed to fight the hunger gnawing in his belly and his groin?

Stuffing his gun in his waistband, McBride reached for his jacket, forced a lid down on the heat and followed her into the thankfully cool night air.

Every head on the porch went up at Alessandra's approach. "Hello." McBride heard the smile in her voice and allowed himself a vague one of his own. Just keep breathing, boys. The blood will start moving again in a minute.

The youngest of the men, seventy-five if he was a day, stood. "Hello back at you, ma'am. I'm Larry Dent. These are my brothers. Folks hereabouts call 'em Curly and Moe."

"What did your parents call them?"

"Among other things, Curly and Moe. Our ma died watching the Stooges on TV." His grin gave way to a shrewd once-over for McBride. "You together?"

Since he didn't mean that in the traveling sense, McBride draped an arm across Alessandra's shoulders. "Married six years. Is there a mechanic in town?"

"Repair shop's mine," the oldest and least mobile of the trio said. "Closed till morning, I'm afraid."

If he was the mechanic, it probably wouldn't matter.

"Engine trouble?" Larry asked. The question was directed at Alessandra.

She fell easily into the part. "If it was that, my husband could fix it, no problem. We went for a bit of a slide to avoid some wildlife and wound up damaging our back end."

The owner, Moe, creaked toward the stairs. "Let's have a look-see, Mr....?"

"Abbott," Alessandra supplied.

She used her mother's surname. Going with it, Mc-

Bride added a cheerful, "Joseph Abbott. My wife's Chastity. Her sister's due to give birth any day now. We need to get to Pennsylvania as soon as possible."

Alessandra watched old Moe descend the stairs. "We heard there was an accident on the main highway, so we took an alternate route this morning and pretty much stayed on it."

"Surprised your truck's not in worse shape, considering." Old Moe finally reached solid ground. "Nice machine, though. Don't see many like it 'round here."

That couldn't be good.

Larry's eyes were glued to Alessandra. "Will you be wanting a motel?"

Her delighted "Is there one nearby?" brought an expression that would have earned the man a fist in the stomach if he'd been a day under seventy.

Pivoting, Larry pointed. "Norm and his ma have a place a mile and half out of town on old 17. It ain't much, but it's clean. You get your gear. I'll run you over, make sure there's someone to check you in. Moe here'll ring up one of his workers. Should know by lunchtime tomorrow if we can help you enough so you can leave town."

Alessandra thanked him, then climbed into the truck and began handing down their backpacks. "Between Norm, his mom and Eddie, I'm not sure I like our chances here, McBride."

He said nothing. He was already envisioning a painful night ahead, a prediction that had nothing to do with his injured shoulder.

They transferred their supplies to a thirty-year-old Dodge pickup. "Ruthie's not partial to pretty women," Larry warned McBride as he squeezed into the seat. "Best all around if you do the talking."

"He usually does," Alessandra said from between them.

McBride knew better than to chuckle. He also knew better than to let himself be distracted by the prospect of spending yet another night in close quarters with her. Last night had been relatively easy. She'd taken the backseat. He'd toughed it out in the front. And used the hole in his shoulder to full advantage whenever his mind had taken a dangerous turn.

Ruthie was planted on a barstool at the front desk when they arrived. She looked almost as pickled as Norman Bates's mother in *Psycho.* As predicted, she ignored Alessandra and dealt solely with McBride.

"Phones don't work." She poked the guest register he was perusing. "Lights and water do. TV reception depends on the wind. Only got one guest—he's in twelve—and some other guy who's renting lot space on account of he likes the smell of incense and I don't. Neither of 'em are here right now, but that doesn't mean you can have yourselves a wild party."

An enormous gray cat emerged from the back room and headed straight for Alessandra. Ruthie's mouth compressed. She tapped stubby fingers and averted her eyes. "If you need food, there's a café in town. Moe's oldest boy does the cooking after he closes up the gas station for the day."

"Sounds good." McBride looked over at Alessandra but noticed she was preoccupied by the cat.

"Your cat has ringworm," she announced, crouching for a closer look. "I can give you the name of something that will take care of the problem."

McBride expected the woman to snarl at the offer. Instead, her wrinkled face took on a suspicious cast. "What's ringworm, and how come you know about it?"

"It's a parasitic infection." She caught the look McBride sent her and added an innocent, "My husband and

I have a farm in Iowa. Our cat had ringworm, but he's better now thanks to the medication."

Ruthie snorted. "I told that no-good doctor something was wrong with Puddles. But would he listen? No, he only does people, not pets." She slammed the register closed, shoved the key at McBride. "You're in seven." She looked to Alessandra. "What needs to be done?"

"There's a shampoo that will take care of the problem. You can order it online. It comes in a concentrate. Follow the instructions, and Puddles will be fine."

The old woman raked her from head to toe. "You sure you two are married, because my Norm has a fondness for dark-haired ladies."

For "ladies," McBride read something a little less flattering. So did Alessandra, but she let it go and pulled the necklace from under her T-shirt.

"My wedding rings." She jingled them. "I've lost weight so they're too loose to wear."

McBride's eyes narrowed. The old woman's face cleared.

"Guess maybe you're okay, then. Write down the cure for Puddles and give it to Larry. He's got that internet. Norm and me don't."

When they emerged, Larry grinned and lowered the truck's rear gate. "Am I seeing things or did Ruthie just crack a smile?"

"Is that what that was?" McBride used his good arm to take out the bags. Then he paused as a prickle of unease slithered across his skin.

His gaze swept the narrow lot. The only vehicles in sight were an old mini school bus turned camper and a Ford Escort from the eighties. Insects chirped in the neighboring trees and leaves rustled overhead. Beyond that and a faulty flickering light in the motel sign, nothing stirred.

"What's wrong?" Alessandra followed his trajectory.

He made a final sweep and set the last of their packs on the ground. "Not sure."

Larry clapped him on his bad shoulder. "Likely you're just worried about your pregnant sister, Joseph."

"My sister." Alessandra printed the name of the ringworm medication and handed him the notepaper. "This is for Puddles. Tell Ruth to follow the instructions, and he'll be as good as new in no time."

Larry seemed curious, but didn't question them further. "I'm assuming you haven't had dinner since you rolled in on old 17," he said as they walked toward the motel room. "I'll run on over to Moe's Café and fetch you a couple of burgers. My brother's boy Morley's only a so-so mechanic, but he can whip up a barbecue sauce that'll make your eyes water for three days. Give me thirty minutes." He chuckled. "Service tends to be a mite slow seeing as Morley's only got three fingers on his right hand."

Small towns, McBride reflected. You had to love 'em.

The motel room was small, poorly lit and boasted a double bed that resembled a canoe. Alessandra gave it and him a meaningful look before grabbing her backpack and heading for the bathroom. "Chastity and I want to freshen up."

He could have pressed her for an explanation of the rings, but since he still had his wedding band and occasionally wore it around his own neck, he decided to let the subject drop. For now.

He prowled the room as Alessandra had Joan's cabin last night. His mind seesawed back and forth between the present and the past.

He'd made their lives difficult from the start with prolonged absences and work-related secrets he couldn't or wouldn't share. But it was his gradual withdrawal that had hurt Alessandra the most. By year three of their marriage, and right near the end of his time as a Chicago cop, he'd been moody and short-tempered, disinclined to talk and pissed off at the world in general.

She'd ridden it out, because she loved him, he assumed, but of course, he hadn't explained much, and eventually she'd stopped asking.

Joining the U.S. marshals had improved his outlook on what he considered to be a failing justice system, but it had also taken him away from her for even longer periods of time.

He stopped the thought there as a single headlight slashed across the partly shaded motel window.

A motorcycle with a beer-bellied driver cruised past, then roared off. The prickle returned and this time snaked down his spine.

He heard the shower running in the background. Music dribbled from a scratchy speaker system. Carrie Underwood was slashing her ex's tires—and Alessandra was wet, naked and less than twenty feet away.

Swearing softly, McBride let his eyes flick to the door. A grim smile played on his lips when he realized he was seriously considering slamming his injured shoulder into the frame in an effort to get his thoughts back in line.

At long last, the water stopped. Releasing a breath, he reached back and pulled the gun from his waistband.

He was setting the weapon and his badge on the nightstand when Alessandra screamed.

Chapter Six

A pair of mud-brown eyes glinted courtesy of the hanging, and currently swinging, bathroom light. Alessandra had hit it with her hand when she'd jumped back. Her heart pounded, her leg muscles wobbled—and those muddy eyes kept right on staring at her.

She didn't realize she'd screamed until the bathroom door opened and McBride appeared behind her. With his gun in one hand, he reached for her arm with the other. He stepped in front of her and although nothing dangerous presented itself, his eyes continued to move around the room. "What happened, Alessandra?"

Her legs firmed up as the last of her fear dissolved.

"It's nothing… Or, well, not much. I opened this door." She tapped a tall cupboard next to the shower. "And there she was."

McBride turned the knob. Once again, Ruthie appeared, in glossy cardboard, large as life and propped up by a heavy metal stand. A motel key dangled from her upraised fingers, and she had a lethal come-in-or-else gleam in her eyes.

"This scared you?" Alessandra caught the trace of humor in McBride's voice and gave him a swat between the shoulder blades.

"You try opening a door to what you think is the linen

closet, find that face staring at you in bad light and see how you react. No wonder they hid it away. A roadside sign like that would terrify kids, adults and probably small animals."

Alessandra was so busy being indignant that it didn't occur to her she was wearing nothing except a skimpy white towel. Until she spied the far less malevolent but equally wicked gleam in McBride's eyes.

"Uh… Hmm." She looked down, let her hand fall from his back. "This is awkward."

"Not from where I'm standing."

"I'm not dressed, McBride."

"I noticed." The gleam became a glitter. He lowered the gun.

Something inside her heart stuttered. "Sex will only mess things up."

He gave a brief laugh. "Darlin', things can't get more messed up than they are at this moment."

He had a point. That didn't make him right.

"I want to keep our relationship simple."

"Not possible, Alessandra. Nothing's ever been simple for us. That's why it all screwed up." A wry smile tugged at his lips. "Or I did."

He was doing it again, holding her with his eyes, making her want to retreat and stand her ground at the same time.

He eased her up against the wall, set a hand next to her head.

"McBride…" she warned through her teeth.

Time stopped right there. Time and every scrap of common sense Alessandra possessed. "God help me," she finally murmured. And with a bolstering breath, she bunched the sides of his open shirt in her fists and dragged his mouth onto hers.

THE HEAT IN THE ROOM, and most definitely in her body, shot up a full one hundred degrees. The kiss was an arousing jolt, surging through her veins like liquid fire.

There never had been anything sweet or slow or tentative between them. Need fused instantly with a hunger Alessandra couldn't seem to obliterate from her memory.

Greed pumped from him into her and back. Desire spiked. His tongue found hers, then plunged in deeper until she groaned.

His fingers tangled in her hair. Her hands slid over his rib cage. He was so hot. His skin was smooth, his muscles sleek and every inch of him was deliciously hard.

She was drowning, she realized, losing herself in the feel of him, in the taste of his mouth and the weight of his body as he crushed her against the wall.

She couldn't breathe, didn't want to. A thousand tiny pulse points snapped to life. His lips explored her face, her cheeks, her eyelids, ran along the side of her neck to her throat.

Another pulse jumped. She wanted to push him onto the floor, to let the animal sounds rising in her throat escape.

Energy zinged around them, a great electric cloud of it. It had a beat.

"Like a drum," she murmured aloud as she let her head fall back so he could kiss her throat.

McBride's lips curved on her skin. "Not a drum, darlin'. There's someone at the door."

Someone… What? Her eyes opened, her head came up. Frustration and a rather unsettling amount of disappointment crept in. "Larry?"

"That'd be my guess."

She wanted to say, "Damn," but turned it into a sigh. "There must be some deep cosmic reason for his timing."

"Yeah." McBride took one last taste of her mouth before backing off. "Morley's not as slow as he thought." Trapping her chin between his thumb and fingers, he stared into her eyes and said, "Don't move."

She didn't, for a full ten seconds after he left. Not because he'd said it, but because her limbs trembled, and that intrigued her as much as it unnerved her. With her brain too rattled to sort any of it out, she simply waited until the sensations passed—more slowly than she would have liked. Then she closed the door on Ruthie's face and let her towel fall to the floor.

It only took her a few minutes to dress and finger fluff her wet hair. Even so, she wasn't surprised to find McBride outside with Larry, talking. She couldn't hear them but she knew they weren't discussing the burgers that sat in a big brown bag on the phone desk.

Sitting down, she unwrapped one. And she had to admit, Three-Finger Morley could cook.

The men talked for several minutes. Finally, with a wave for McBride and a broad wink through the window for her, Larry started off.

"You moved," McBride said when he came back in. But she knew his mind was miles away and already in overdrive. "Cheech is dead."

She almost missed the relevance, until she remembered where they were and why. "Rory's contact?" At his nod, she frowned. "That's not good."

Rather than unwrap the second burger, McBride took a bite of hers. "It's not completely bad, either. Larry recognized a picture of Rory."

"When did Larry see him?"

"Late yesterday. Rory bought a six-pack from Moe and asked for directions to Creek Road."

"Where Cheech lives—lived."

"He went crazy and died last April. Hydrophobia."

Rabies. Alessandra winced. "Did they catch the animal that bit him?"

Taking another bite, he glanced into the bag. "I didn't ask."

"Of course not… Uh, McBride, wait a minute." She snagged his sleeve and motioned at the window. "There's someone in the bushes over there."

He followed her line of sight, then set a hand on her hip and eased her away from the glass. "Get our stuff."

She didn't hesitate, simply pushed everything that was loose into their backpacks and hooked her fingers through the looped tops. "What now?"

"Don't move—and I mean it this time."

His kept his eyes on the bushes. "Come on," he said under his breath. "Let me see who you are."

Maybe the bush man heard him because a shot blasted across the gravel lot and blew out half the motel room window.

Alessandra knew a high-powered rifle when she heard one. She ducked.

Already on one knee, McBride returned fire twice.

The bushes rustled, then shook apart. A man, doubled over and clutching two guns, darted out briefly, only to vanish in the shadows.

"I might have hit him." Taking Alessandra's arm, McBride drew her toward the door. "This is the only way out. When I say go, run. Keep low and stay behind me. I'll cover you." He withdrew a second gun.

"Are you ready?"

"Yes."

He used the barrel of a gun to point east. "Head for that old school bus. Get to the side that's not lit by the motel."

She prayed he wasn't planning to hot-wire the thing. But they'd need a vehicle, and there didn't appear to be a lot of choice.

He opened the door. "Okay, go."

Thoughts rushed through her head as she ran. Someone had printed California or Bust in red on the side of the bus. Nothing about the words or the vehicle reassured her, because it was a bus, after all, and because Eddie was close by with a rifle and likely very little patience at this point.

The silence remained unbroken until she reached the painted side. Then Eddie let loose, McBride returned fire and everything around them seemed to tilt.

The sound was deafening, especially when McBride squeezed the trigger.

She saw the lobby door open and Ruthie's terrified face emerge. McBride shouted for her to get back inside. As a fresh round of bullets shattered the night, she did just that and extinguished the light.

Alessandra scrabbled through her pack for Dr. Lang's .45. It wasn't until she tried to load it that she realized the good doctor had bought the wrong bullets. "Figures." She nudged McBride between shots. "Give me your second gun."

"Can you shoot?"

"I'm a farmer's daughter, McBride."

"Mennonite farmer's daughter."

"Farmers kill and cull when necessary. I just made a point of always missing."

Another flurry of bullets erupted. Alessandra ducked

instinctively, then almost jumped out of her skin when a hand descended on her shoulder.

She knocked it away, whirled—and stared in disbelief.

"Larry?"

"You bet." Reaching past her, he tapped McBride's back. "I heard the first shots, saw someone running for cover."

"Yeah, we got that much ourselves. Did you happen to notice how many weapons the guy was packing?"

"Saw three good-size guns and pretty sure some blood on the front of his shirt. I reckon he's hunkered down in that gully behind those two big pines."

But McBride shook his head. "Shots are coming from that stand of trees next to the lobby."

"Does it matter?" Alessandra asked in a whisper. "Either way, we're trapped behind this bus."

"No, we're not." Larry pointed his finger. "My truck's parked at this end of the motel. I stopped to have a chat with Ruthie and heard the ruckus as I was pulling out. I figured you must be in trouble, so I came back."

McBride glanced at the motel. "Okay, we go on three. Stay behind me and down."

Once again, Alessandra's world tipped toward the surreal. Her feet felt like lead, and everything unfolded in superslow motion.

Bullets peppered the air in both directions. The idea that something wasn't quite right flitted through her head, but it came and went so quickly she couldn't examine it.

"There's my truck," Larry wheezed behind them. "Get in. We'll lose him in the dark, circle 'round to my place."

McBride negated the plan. "It's too dangerous for us to stay with you."

The old man spun the steering wheel like a pro. "What's your plan, then?"

"Lose Eddie, and I'll tell you. Here you go, darlin'." Belatedly, he handed his backup gun to Alessandra. "Keep the safety on, and don't shoot to miss."

She tucked the Sig Sauer in the pack she'd instinctively grabbed and sent him a level look. "Your work sucks, McBride." Which was, she reflected, the one constant in their lives.

"I knew you weren't being truthful back at Moe's station." Larry zigzagged along a series of nearly invisible roadways. "Then, when you asked about Cheech... You're a cop, aren't you?"

"Was," Alessandra corrected. "Back when he valued his life."

"She gets cranky when she doesn't get enough sleep." McBride looked behind them. "Can you take us to Cheech's place?"

"We're almost there. What about the fella who's after you? Won't he think to look for you there?"

"I doubt if he knows about it."

He doubted? Alessandra stared at him. "I'm taking an awful lot on faith here, McBride."

"It's one of your best qualities."

"You two really married?" Giving the wheel a hard, two-handed crank-over, Larry started down a steep incline.

Alessandra dug in with both feet. "It's a long story."

"She means yes." McBride checked their tail again as he filled Larry in on their identities and their dilemma. "You're risking a lot for us, Larry."

"Well, hell, I'm seventy-eight, and the highlight of most days is a game of checkers with my brothers."

Alessandra smiled. "He means he's bored."

"Stiff as old Cheech when Morley found him snout down alongside the creek bed." He stopped his truck to let them out. "See that ridge there? You go up and over, then head south about five hundred yards. You spot an old '47 Airstream trailer, you're there."

And twenty minutes of hard slogging later, they were.

Alessandra's nerves were stretched well past their breaking point by the time the dried-up creek bed led them around a final bend. She swiped at spiderwebs and hoped neither of them had stepped in the ants' nest her flashlight had discovered.

She played her beam in a cautious arc. "You know there are mountain lions in these hills, right?"

"Think of them as a step up from Eddie."

"Speaking of, something wasn't right about that— whatever you want to call it back there."

"It was a shoot-out, Alessandra, and I know."

"Good, then explain it to me, because all I got was a feeling, not the specifics."

"I'll let you know when it clicks." After clearing away a huge web, he gestured forward. "There's the trailer."

It looked more like a rusty tin can to her, but as long as Eddie wasn't there, she really didn't care.

When McBride remained stationary, she glanced up at him. "Aren't we going in?"

"Switch off your light."

She angled it down and complied. "What?"

"Don't you hear it?"

"All I hear are insects, frogs…" Then her senses tuned in. "And a motor."

"Yeah, a motor." McBride regarded the dented rear

section of the Airstream. "Coming from the trailer of a man who died four months ago."

EDDIE COLLAPSED in his truck, breathing in grunts and sweating like a pig.

How the crap had this become a triangular shoot-fest? Had the geezer with the pickup been helping McBride and the lady doc, or was Rory on some kind of drug that erased yellow backbones, because he'd sure as hell never been one to plant and confront before.

Peeling his shirt away with care, Eddie examined the bullet hole in his side. No exit wound meant the frigging thing was still inside him. That made them even, he supposed, him and McBride. They'd both shot at the phantom in the trees for good measure. McBride more than him, but maybe one of them had gotten lucky and the rifle guy had taken a hit, too.

Whatever. Getting back on his feet was the priority here. The phantom could be popped later—unless it was Rory, in which case, he'd whack McBride and the pretty vet, belt Rory a good one in the chops, then see to it that the rest of big sister's orders were carried out as specified.

Megabucks, Eddie thought, and a couple weeks in a banana republic would send the pain in his side packing fast enough. Either way, he had plenty of ammo and a real itchy trigger finger right now.

Looking down at the blood that continued to ooze, he gave a rusty laugh and reached for the bourbon he kept under the seat. The first slug helped him relax. Halfway through, the bottleneck slipped from his fingers. That's when he looked around and noticed the shadows falling over him had suddenly gotten a lot deeper....

Chapter Seven

"There's no one here, Alessandra."

She believed him but maintained her position in the doorway of the spartanly decked out Airstream trailer. "Someone was here," she pointed out. "The fridge is running and the fuel tank on the generator's half-full."

"Could be a vagrant." However, from the way Mc-Bride was looking around, she knew he didn't believe that.

"Could also be Rory," she remarked. "Either way, we're left with a big question mark. All we can say for sure is that Eddie was at the motel tonight, Rory was at Moe's filling station yesterday and someone was in the home of his dead contact as recently as today. It's your dime, McBride. What do we do now?"

McBride studied a cigarette butt plucked from an overflowing ashtray. "This is Rory's brand."

"I guess it's not a vagrant, then. That still doesn't tell me what we do now."

He picked up and sniffed a fast-food container. "We lock the door, camp out until morning."

"And if Rory shows up?"

"Then I'll have him, and we'll head back to Chicago via Rapid City."

"Aren't you forgetting Eddie?"

"Trust me, he's at the forefront of my mind." Mc-Bride's mouth quirked. "Pretty much."

She couldn't help laughing. "You know you're sick, right?"

He shrugged as he stood. "I'm a man. My mind has layers. You hover near the top. Lock the door, Alessandra."

She leaned against the frame, eyeing him with amused suspicion. "Seriously."

He grinned back at her. "I'm hungry."

Her brows went up.

"For food, I'm sorry to say. So park that spectacular butt of yours, and tell me there's something edible in your backpack."

Because his pack, she recalled, was still at the motel.

"Don't get your hopes up," she warned him as she walked over to the table. "There isn't much." She hunted, produced a square box and sighed. "One slightly squished pie, a handful of granola bars and half a bottle of orange juice."

"I got all the heavy stuff, huh?"

"You're the one who's ripped."

When his eyes darkened to storm gray, one word echoed in her head. *Oops.* Very wrong thing to say.

He started toward her, his eyes raking over her. "You look damn fit to me, Alessandra."

She pulled out the serrated knife. "Lose the gleam, McBride. Just cut the pie, and tell me what we do if Rory's a no-show and Eddie doesn't figure out where we are."

He was close enough now to affect her breathing, but he didn't touch her. He only stared at her for a long moment, before extending his hand, palm up.

"I need your BlackBerry."

"Right." She rummaged through one of the zipped

compartments. "You're lucky I'm a tolerant…" A frown knit her brow. "Rifle shot…"

He began punching buttons on the BlackBerry she'd absently produced. "Not following you, darlin'."

"I finally realized what didn't seem right about the shoot-out at the motel." Her mind skipped backward, frame by frame. "The window was blown out with a high-powered rifle. But when we saw Eddie running from the bushes, he was only carrying a pair of guns. You could say he dropped the rifle, except we heard it again a few seconds later."

McBride's gaze traveled sideways. "The shots Larry heard came from the gully across from the motel. The ones I heard came from the trees next to it."

"Can't be in two places at one time," Alessandra reasoned. "Assuming you're both right, there must have been two shooters." She bit her lower lip. "Eddie *and* Rory?"

"You don't know Rory. Two hit men, maybe."

But that seemed inefficient to Alessandra. "What about one guy sent to kill you, and another to bring Rory back? The two could have met, decided to work together and split the money."

McBride toyed with the idea, then returned his attention to the BlackBerry. "Let's see what I can find out."

A chill feathered along Alessandra's spine. The trailer had taken on an eerie ambience. She regarded a small wall clock whose hands were stuck at 3:10 a.m. Even so, it ticked and ticked and struggled to move. Like a bomb with a faulty timer. One that could tick forever—or go off at any second.

SHE WAS ON A BUS, speeding along a tree-lined road. Needle-sharp bullets, like slivered glass, jackhammered the sides as they passed. It was only a matter of time before one of those slivers penetrated the rusty metal.

She felt her pulse accelerate and a scream lodge itself in her throat. Then one of the bullets split the side of the bus, aiming right at her. She closed her eyes and took her last breath....

She woke with a gasp in her throat, rolled to get away from the shots from her nightmare and wound up facedown on the floor. Rather, on something lumpy. Something that moved.

Her eyes flew open, and the gasp escaped. She scrambled to her knees. "McBride!"

"I'm right here." He gripped her waist, held her firmly in place. "You're kneeling on my stomach, Alessandra. A few inches lower, and I'll be a sexual cripple for life."

"What? Oh."

Realization dawned in stages. It was McBride underneath her. They were in a trailer and the glass bullets she thought she'd heard were merely raindrops pummeling the roof.

"Knee," McBride reminded when she tried to climb off, a feat made doubly difficult by the fact that she was tangled in her sleeping bag.

She shimmied up and off, squinted at the wall clock— 3:10 a.m. and holding.

Sweeping the hair from her face, she attempted to separate her hideous dream from the gruesome reality. Then she spied McBride's bandage, and concern blotted out fear. She reached over to tug the edge free. "How's your shoulder? Ouch, ouch, ouch."

"What is it?" He came upright instantly.

Hissing, she ditched the sleeping bag and pounded her left ankle. "My foot's asleep."

He fell back on his elbow. "Lucky foot."

"You can eighty-six the sarcasm, McBride. Rory's buddy's army cot is straight out of a World War I trench. The floor can't be any more uncomfortable."

He grinned when she flexed her foot and winced. "You need to apply pressure, Alessandra." Catching her by the calf, he used his thumbs on her instep and arch. Almost immediately, the needles and pins began to recede.

Resting her weight on her hands, she welcomed the relief and at the same time tried not to acknowledge the warm sensations snaking up her leg.

"You'd have made a great massage therapist, McBride."

"I'll keep that in mind if the marshal thing doesn't pan out."

She regarded him through her lashes. He was such an incredible man to look at, the quintessential male to her mind. Except for the death wish so many believed he carried around inside. Deep inside, yet omnipresent, as if he really did blame himself for his father's actions, or at least believed it was his responsibility to atone for them.

That was ridiculous, of course, but she knew it went that way sometimes. Children watched, assimilated and slowly became what they saw. In McBride's case, what he'd seen, absorbed and become had taken on a life of its own. The lower his father had sunk, the more determined he'd been to soar. Unfortunately, he'd done so with the same reckless abandon as the man he'd resolved never to emulate.

Although he didn't look up, a slow smile formed on McBride's lips. "You're psychoanalyzing me, aren't you?"

"No." She lowered her lashes farther. "Maybe." When

he squeezed her foot, she jerked and opened her eyes. "Okay, yes. I keep hoping that death wish inside you will disappear, but it never does."

"If that were true, last night's shoot-out wouldn't have gone the way it did."

"You mean you'd have seen it through to its conclusion, one way or the other."

"I would have hung at the motel a while longer," he agreed. His eyes met hers. "I don't want to die. I'm just willing to go right to the edge for what I believe. Last night, getting you out of there was more important than going another few rounds with Eddie."

"And that second shooter."

"Yeah."

His eyes assumed that remote cast they got when his mind slid out of the moment. To keep it from wandering too far and her own from straying in the wrong direction, she shook her foot free and adopted a crossed-legged position on the sleeping bag.

A deceptive smile played on his mouth. "You look good in your boxer shorts and tank, darlin', but unless you want a rerun and then some of last night's bathroom scene, you should think about getting dressed. And yes, the shower works."

Despite the sexual overtones and his lazy drawl, she smiled. "I'm not that predictable, McBride, or that fanatical."

"Uh-huh." When she didn't move, he raised a brow. "Shower or rerun. Choice is yours, Alessandra. For about three more seconds."

She took two of them to think, then went with her better sense and stood. "I should never have told you I was moving to Rapid City."

He watched her collect her bathroom supplies, but

beyond that didn't move. "You never told me how the relocation came about or why. You had a good job in one of the best animal hospitals in Chicago, and I'd already promised to keep my distance."

She moved a shoulder, pulled out the last of the clean towels they'd bought in Dead Lake. "Joan's sister, Lottie, worked at the same animal hospital. I met Joan through Lottie, and Dr. Lang through Joan. I wanted a change, he wanted a partner. Things just sort of fell into place from there." She paused with a hand on the bathroom door. "Not to change the subject, but do we have a plan for today, because I assume we're not going to be hanging around here for much of it?"

When McBride reached for her BlackBerry, she sighed. Talk about sexy in boxers...

"You'll know when I know, Alessandra." Vague amusement entered his tone. "Don't worry about the hot water. I'll go with a cold shower this morning."

Alessandra took that as her cue to leave. And not dwell, she promised herself, because God knew she'd done plenty of that already and still hadn't worked out a thing in her head.

She had a life, she had a practice, she had friends and a house. Okay, she also had a bull breeder who'd been angry enough to threaten her. But at least he hadn't been the one wielding a rifle outside Ruthie's motel last night.

The water was still running warm when she finished up her abbreviated morning ritual. She emerged from the bathroom fully dressed in jeans, a snug white T-shirt and her new hiking boots. She knew there was no way McBride's truck would be fixed and, with Eddie in town, lingering in Ben's Creek wasn't an option.

"Joan says her nephew and his girlfriend were bushwhacked in her Dead Lake cabin two nights ago." Mc-

Bride traded Alessandra the BlackBerry for her damp towel. "She thinks I'm into something more dangerous than usual, and you're supposed to tell me to make sure I know she'll bust my balls—literally, she swears—if anything happens to you." His eyes took on a wicked gleam. "I gather Joan's not aware of your prowess with firearms."

"I could shoot an apple off your head and send her some before and after pictures." When he merely grinned and closed the bathroom door, she added, "I didn't think so."

Five minutes later, McBride was back in fresh jeans and an open, untucked plaid shirt.

He looked like a hot lumberjack. He took a drink from the orange juice bottle in her hand, then turned his head and set a finger on her lips. "Someone's coming."

Let it be a bear, she prayed, and took the gun he gave her.

They stood one, two against the wall. McBride watched through the window next to him. "Footsteps are heavy. It's not Eddie."

She couldn't see around his arm or read anything other than his trap-waiting-to-spring body language.

When he swore, her muscles cinched into knots. They tightened even more when he said, "Stay inside." Then, catching her arms, he dropped a hot, hard kiss on her lips, and took off, without sound or warning, through the door.

SHE WANTED TO PUNCH someone, specifically McBride for scaring her half to death. As for his kiss, which had startled her into immobility, that just plain pissed her off.

She had no similar feelings of malice toward Larry Dent, perpetrator of the heavy footsteps, who now stood with them outside the trailer. How could she be upset with a man who was doing everything possible, and more than he safely should, to help them?

"I brought your pack," he told McBride, "and stocked you up on the supplies I figured you'd need most." His twinkling eyes told Alessandra he was enjoying himself immensely. "We'll get to the what and where of that later. I got Morley to take my old Dodge out and run it around town. Then I snuck over to Moe's place and woke up the big black monster he's way too weak to drive these days. Don't be thinking slick, shiny and all-powerful, but don't be fooled by the dings and scrapes, either. Moe's monster truck's got muscle and stamina, and, at this moment, a lot more going for it than the truck you rolled up in. Questions so far?"

"Yeah," McBride tucked his gun away. "You wanna sign on with the U.S. marshals?"

"Shave thirty years off my birth date, and you got a deal." Larry eyed the bunched gray clouds overhead. "Rain came down hard in the night, but me and Morley took a walk around the motel this morning between showers. We saw traces of blood. Could be animal, could be human, but it was mostly in the gully where I told you the shots came from."

"Eddie?" Alessandra suggested, and McBride nodded.

"Anything else?" McBride asked Larry.

"We found some slugs and bagged them for you. Three of Ruthie's windows took hits, so she's a little steamed about that."

"McBride'll mail her a check," Alessandra promised, and earned herself a level look that brought a laugh to her throat.

It was probably hysteria, she reflected. To fight it, she trudged around the trailer and disengaged the generator.

"I heard once that weird stuff happens in clumps," Larry was commenting when she returned. "Maybe it does at that. We got shots fired, we got blood, we got broken windows, we got a scared hippie camper who hightailed it in the middle of the night, then to top it off, we got a break-in at Doc Dyer's place."

McBride hoisted Alessandra's backpack as they began their trek along the creek. "Home or office?"

"One and the same in Ben's Creek."

"What was stolen?"

"Bandages, a couple sharp instruments, two bottles of Jack Black."

"Sounds like someone—back to Eddie again—needs a metaphorical bullet to bite." Alessandra sidestepped a large puddle, grateful that the rain had stopped. "Were there any witnesses?"

Larry chuckled. "I hate to admit it, but we generally roll up our sidewalks by nine o'clock. One more thing, though." When he started to puff, she dropped back a pace to observe. "Ruthie wants to know, after the hoopla's over and the right people get caught and sent to jail, is this story gonna be in *People* magazine? If it is, she says to tell her ahead of time so she can get her hair done."

Alessandra couldn't help it. The picture of Ruthie with "done" hair made her laugh. It even coaxed a grin out of McBride and a wheezy chortle out of Larry.

"The monster's parked over the ridge," the old man said. "Morley'll be waiting for me in my truck at the crossroad." He accepted the hands Alessandra and McBride offered for the climb. "Don't know if *People* will work out, but you be sure and let me know how things go for you two from here. Your truck'll be ready for sure by midweek. I want to hear all the details when you come to pick it up."

Alessandra pulled hard so the old man wouldn't over-exert. Then she halted and hitched in a sharp breath when she spied a shimmer of movement on a boulder twenty yards behind Larry's shoulder.

Chapter Eight

"Stop glaring at me, McBride." Alessandra felt his eyes on her as she completed her text to Joan. "Nothing happened. We're all safe and that mountain lion that didn't attack us is probably reaffirming his territory as we speak."

He shot her a dark look. "Or sleeping off the breakfast we were fortunate not to be. I know a thing or two about big cats, Alessandra. Humans aren't their first choice as meals go, but it happens."

"I didn't expect you to let him take a bite out of anyone, only to give him a moment to decide. He decided we weren't worth attacking, or he didn't want to take on three of us. End of problem. Pothole ahead."

"I see it."

Their route today involved more semiabandoned roads and highways. McBride hadn't spoken much for the first three hours of their drive. Yes, he was annoyed because she hadn't wanted him to shoot the mountain lion, but she sensed that wasn't the cause of his protracted silence.

A glance at the dashboard clock told her it was almost 1:00 p.m. She decided he'd mulled long enough.

"You're trying to get inside Rory's head, aren't you?"

He rested an arm on the open window. "In a way. I'm

also thinking about an email I got before Larry showed up. It said, Try Loden."

"Is that a person or a place?"

"It's a place in seventeen states, one of them being Wyoming."

She regarded the distant swell of mountains. Not the Black Hills, according to McBride's laptop map. These were the Laramie Mountains.

"I'm never going to get home, am I?"

"Good things come to those who wait, Alessandra. I'll have you back in Rapid City by Christmas."

"Hey, I'm open for sugarcoating here. You do realize that unless Loden's population is under twenty, you could have a very difficult time finding Rory through what I assume is another contact."

"It's Cheech's cousin."

"Ah. Does he have a name?"

"Billy."

She waited for more, didn't get it and arched a brow. "That's it? Just Billy?"

He adjusted the cowboy hat that Larry had included with the supplies he'd crammed into the truck. "Billy's better than nothing, and on a positive note, it's possible we'll get to Loden on Rory's heels, which is closer than we've been so far."

"Uh-huh. What makes you think that?"

A small smile played on his mouth. "Gut feeling, darlin'. He'll be confused right now, on the verge of panic. Unless he was one of the shooters, which I doubt, he has to know he has two, possibly three people after him. It's also a good bet he's running out of cash. I make it a point to know my quarry. Planning for the long haul's not Rory's strong suit."

"And using an ATM would be like sending up a flare."

"To more than one person."

"What does that leave?"

"Theft or some other kind of decent-size score. My source says Rory's got a weakness for craps and black-jack." For the third time in a minute, McBride's gaze flicked to the rearview mirror.

Twisting around, Alessandra regarded the two-lane road. "Is someone behind us?"

"A couple big rigs, maybe a smaller truck. They're keeping their distance."

As Alessandra knew she should be doing, but foolishly wasn't. Not with enough determination, anyway. Her thoughts kept taking detours, dredging up memories, flashing pictures of other times and places. A skiing trip in McBride's home state of Colorado. Their honeymoon adventure in Africa. A beach vacation in the Bahamas.

The last memory made her sad. Her mother would have loved McBride, but then her mother had possessed a huge capacity for love.

She must have to have married a man like Alessandra's father.

Her brow furrowed when he checked the mirror again. "McBride, what's behind us that's riveting your attention so completely? All I see is a long stretch of nearly empty road."

"The land's opened up, Alessandra. My guess is Eddie has a faster truck than us, and if that blood Larry and Morley saw this morning was his, he'll be on a tear."

Not a pretty picture, she decided with a shiver. "Tell you what. I'll watch, you drive."

The sun peeked out the farther west they went. A

single-seater plane dusting masses of swaying cornfields glimmered in the distance. She'd had a date with Cary Grant and a similar cornfield back in another lifetime, one where sanity had more or less prevailed.

Moe's big black truck had a radio that worked. She turned it on and tuned it to a country music station.

In his thorough way, Larry had sent along sandwiches, cookies and bottled water. They ate while they drove. Alessandra alternated between scanning for trucks and stealing glances at McBride's inscrutable profile.

She did not want to jump him, she promised herself, then released a breath and let her head drop onto the seat back. "Yeah, right," she murmured. "Just call me Pinocchio."

Beside her, McBride chuckled. "Talking to yourself means you need exercise and fresh air. The truck needs gas. We can get both in Rosewater."

Unfortunately, reaching Rosewater required thirty more minutes of highway driving followed by an obscure dogleg and five miles of low hills and shallow valleys.

Very slowly, cropland gave way to thin clumps of trees and, beyond that, a scattering of weathered houses. On the edge of town, Alessandra spotted a tired supermarket and—what a surprise—another run-down rest stop, this one with three fuel pumps and an attached café.

"Not a rosebush or drop of water in sight," she said, noting the irony of the town's name. Sliding out, she stretched her arms and arched her body sideways. "It does feel good to move, though."

"Looks even better." McBride came up behind her. As he had before, he stuck his hat on her head.

She tipped her sunglasses down. "You know this unobtrusive thing never works, right?"

"First time for everything." He squinted through the café window. "It's not busy. Want a burger and fries?"

"I just had a ham sandwich."

"Sign says there's homemade gravy."

"Your arteries must hate you, McBride. I'll pass. Larry sent another message. I'll read it while you fill up on grease."

Reaching past her, he shoved the creaking door open. "Stay where I can see you."

"Bathroom doesn't count. Otherwise, I'll do my best."

When she followed him into the café, it took a moment for her eyes to adjust. The café's worn wooden walls belonged to another century and boasted equally old photos of bedraggled prospectors, dusty cowboys and trappers hefting lines of pelts.

Not very appetizing, she thought. But history was history, and not much could be worse in her opinion than the sight of the whippy female currently slapping burgers on the grill while a cigarette dangled from her mouth.

Deliberately averting her eyes, Alessandra turned to read Larry's text.

He and Morley had apparently tromped around the motel, beating bushes and searching every hidey-hole they could find. They'd discovered tire tracks under a wide rock ledge and more bloodstains, but nothing that told them what they wanted to know.

When Alessandra glanced up, she saw a man at one of the tables picking his teeth and leering in her direction. She circled him and kept to the shadows.

The grill sizzled and spat. Country music twanged. Flies and mosquitoes buzzed. Three teenage girls and a boy sauntered in with a droopy basset hound at their heels.

Two of the girls detached from the group and headed for the counter where McBride sat chatting with a man in a stained white shirt. The girls giggled. McBride glanced over, smiled, then returned to his conversation with the man.

That had to sting, Alessandra reflected. Gorgeous stranger sees a lot of skin, and his eyes don't drop out of his head.

She continued to wander. The toothpick man thumped his empty beer glass down on the table and let out a loud belch.

Alessandra slid her BlackBerry into her shoulder bag and sighed. "You bring me to the nicest places, McBride," she murmured.

She didn't see a thing and only heard one quick foot-step before a hand slammed across her mouth and another one wrenched her left arm up behind her back.

"Move with me, lady," said a man's voice behind her as he jerked her around and shoved her forward.

She hadn't noticed the hallway at the rear of the café. Short and narrow, it had a sharp right turn that led to a door. He booted it open and carried her, struggling and kicking, into a graveyard of broken appliances, metal garbage cans and a derelict cube van with no wheels.

"Inside, hellcat," he snarled. Unwilling to wait, he hefted her through the open back doors.

It wasn't Eddie, her terrified mind realized. She remembered his voice. The rifle guy, maybe?

The man gave one last mighty shove. He released her arm but sank his hand into her hair before pushing her head into the metal wall. Spinning her around, he yanked.

"Stay the hell away from me," he grated through his teeth. "Do what it takes, but get McBride off my ass."

Alessandra's head swam. He had something long and silver pressed to her windpipe now. A knife?

A single ray of light sliced across his filthy moon face. Shock and a fresh bolt of fear coursed through her. "You're Rory, aren't you?"

"Who else d'you think?" He shook her. "I don't want to kill you, okay? I never meant to kill Laverne. She got hold of my gun. I only ever carried one because— Aw, what does it matter?"

"It doesn't." Needle-sharp splinters of pain caused Alessandra's voice to hitch. "It doesn't."

"Then make McBride stop and go back to Chicago. Hell, sure, kill Eddie first, I don't care about him. I just want to be gone. That's what Casey wants, too, don't you see? Eddie's after McBride, not me. McBride dies, I slip away. Poof, gone forever. Family stays whole. Secrets stay secret. Everyone's happy. So go home and live. You keep chasing me, you and McBride'll die. Simple, simple."

Her head cleared just enough for her to counter, "If you want McBride to go home, why did you shoot at us last night with an assault rifle?"

"A what? Are you nuts?" He barked out a laugh. "I'm crap with guns, lady. It's all hype. My sister put out the word, and suddenly I'm a ruthless sharpshooter. Big, bad Rory Simms. Built like an ox, with brains and balls to match." He stuck his face close to hers. "I wanted to write poetry."

Poetry? She struggled to think. "What if you're wrong about what your sister wants?"

Doubt flickered in his eyes, but he brushed it off. "Doesn't matter if I'm wrong. Point is, I get away, everything's cool. McBride stays on my tail, Eddie stays on his."

"So Eddie'll just go away if McBride backs off?"

"Yeah. Eventually. Okay, sure, he'll be pissed, but when a new job comes along, he'll forget about McBride and go with the cash. And we're back to everyone wins."

The café door opened. Rory's head snapped around. Cursing, he tossed Alessandra aside and bolted. She heard a shocked "What the hell...?" and glimpsed the teenage boy fumbling with his fly as he leaned against the door.

Here was the reason, she thought through a haze, the raw bones of why she and McBride had split. In his out of control world, a train wreck like Rory Simms was no different than the bus crash that had almost ended her life.

FOR THE SECOND time in as many days, McBride had to track Alessandra down in a rest-stop bathroom. He'd given her five minutes out of sight. That was three minutes longer than he'd intended, but some guy with a toothpick had been harassing one of the teenage girls, and he couldn't pretend not to see it. Unfortunately, the guy had a surly nature, ham-size fists and a good dozen under his belt. He hadn't backed down willingly.

The bathroom doors read Hers and His. They both read Out of Order. Knowing Alessandra, he was about to nudge Hers open, anyway, when the boy he'd seen earlier stumbled in, flushed and cradling a bloody arm.

"Guy's a freak," he exclaimed. "He was trying to get some ass in the back of that old van that used to be a chicken truck. Man, there's hen crap all over the floor...."

The boy kept going, but McBride was already out the back door.

Alessandra plowed into his chest, more specifically into his injured shoulder. The impact had him seeing stars for a moment. He toughed it out, wrapped one hand around her arm and tipped her head up with the other. "Are you hurt? What happened?"

She bunched his shirt and shook. "I'm not hurt. It was Rory. He ran when the kid came out. I don't think he has a gun. He was holding a knife on me, McBride, a butter knife. He dropped it in the van before he took off."

McBride followed the direction of her eyes, but didn't release her. "You need to be inside."

"What? No." Having apparently gathered her wits, she shook him again. "McBride, Rory's here. In Rose-water. At this rest stop. You'll never get a better chance to catch him."

He felt the tearing in his gut.

"Go." She pushed him. "I'm not hurt. Get him." When he still didn't move, she made an exasperated sound. "If you won't, I will."

He stopped her easily, angled her toward the door. "Go into the main room and stay there. Check out the kid. He's bleeding. You've got my backup. If you see Rory before I do, use it."

He closed the café door himself, then drew his gun and started around the side of the building.

In McBride's mind Rory's big ugly face got bigger and uglier the farther he ran. The bastard had put his hands on Alessandra. He'd pay for that, along with everything else. Rape wasn't Rory's deal as far as McBride knew, but that didn't mean he wouldn't stoop to it under the right circumstances and in a particularly nasty frame of mind.

A hundred yards ahead, he emerged in a clearing rimmed with trees and scraggly bushes. Beyond it stood another cornfield.

He slowed, scanned, listened.

Birds and insects chirped, buzzed and hummed. The sun blazed overhead. Dry cornstalks rustled. He smelled dust in the air and the pungent odor of diesel fuel.

But nothing human stirred.

McBride's gaze went to the only visible road. He was heading toward it when someone inside the café screamed.

Chapter Nine

"It's a scratch." Alessandra used her calm, professional tone to soothe the screaming girl. "A deep one, but nothing to worry about."

The injured boy, pale and trembling from mild shock, nodded. The girl with him alternated between teary hyperventilation and fearful gulping whimpers.

"There's so much blood," she warbled. "And I see bone…"

Her eyes rolled back, and she hit the floor at the feet of her frightened friends. The cook marched over. Emitting a tsk of disgust, she stabbed the air with her spatula.

"Bonnie Lynn, you pick yourself up and stop being such a drama queen. Your daddy's a butcher, God's sake. And you, boy, you let the lady doc here do what's necessary so we can all get back to eatin'." A slamming door halted her tirade. "Well, hello there again, cutie."

Alessandra looked up to find McBride leaning against the doorframe watching them. He was alone, so he hadn't caught Rory. She recognized the glint of annoyance in his eyes.

"Got away, huh?" Alessandra asked as she returned to deal with the boy's arm. The long abrasion showed a little fat but no bone.

Pushing off, McBride gave the toothpick man a steady look and the boy's abrasion a glance. "I imagine his vehicle was parked in the bushes next to the gas station." He nodded toward the boy. "Will this take long?"

"Ten minutes. There's a doctor in town, so I'm not going to stitch, only wrap. He cut it on a piece of metal when Ro—the guy who grabbed me knocked him down." She heard a soft beep in her shoulder bag. "Incoming text, McBride."

"Burger and fries coming up," the cook promised with a flirty smile. "On the house and smothered in my special gravy."

Alessandra was tying a knot in the gauze when McBride caught her eye.

"Make it a fast cleanup, darlin'. We still have some driving to do, and a mystery to work on as we go."

"You'll live," she told the boy. "But get to your doctor as soon as possible… What?" she asked McBride, who was perched in a deceptively easy manner on one of the high counter stools.

He angled the BlackBerry so she could see Larry's message.

It read: Me and Morley found the body of Edward Louis Rickard five miles from town. Looks like he bled to death in his truck. Doc Dyer recognized the bullet straight off. ELR was shot and killed by someone using a high-powered rifle.…

"So, EDDIE, AKA Edward Louis Rickard, is dead," Alessandra stated. "I know this sounds callous, but whether his agenda was to kill you so he could bring Rory back to his sister, or kill you so Rory could get away, the fact is, for us, it's a major problem solved. Rory's a different story. Whatever he knows or doesn't know, hears or doesn't hear, isn't it a little crazy to think he'd still be heading for Loden?" She clamped both hands on the dash as they blew past an eighteen-wheeler. "God, McBride, slow down."

Ruts and potholes were no longer a concern. Right now, it was all about speed. McBride had Moe's truck flying along the interstate. At best, she'd describe the current landscape as a brown blur.

"He's trying to outthink us, Alessandra."

"By going where we expect him to go."

"Which, in his mind, is the last place he'd expect us to look for him."

She made a leapfrog motion with her index finger. "Logically speaking, wouldn't he be farther ahead to scratch Billy from the contact list regardless of what he thinks we're thinking, and move on to whoever's next in line?"

"Logically speaking, yes. But he exposed himself to you when there was no need for it. That's desperation. Rory might or might not hear about Eddie—probably won't, given his current state of panic—but either way, my money's on Loden and his limited talent for reverse psychology."

Since she didn't know enough about the man to argue, Alessandra pried her hands off the dash and sat cautiously back. Another round of local country music allowed her to check out her neglected weekend emails rather than the road or McBride.

She'd already opened everything from Joan and Larry. Medical supply companies could wait. A pair of friends in Rapid City wanted to do a girls' night before Labor Day. Several people had sent pictures of their healthy or convalescing pets. She received thank-you cards, animated happy faces and one exploding heart that rained love and meows over the screen.

Two dinner invitations followed, from men whose faces she couldn't bring to mind. Made sense since she was sitting next to the reason why.

So shallow, she thought. Or at least she thought she'd merely thought it. The upward tilt of McBride's lips suggested the words had actually slipped out.

"I hope you're not talking about me."

"I wish, but no. Though I often wonder how my life would have gone if I'd married Toby, the boy next door, and settled into the farming lifestyle."

"Seriously?"

"Yes." Then her mind formed a picture. "No." She scrolled through more messages on her BlackBerry. "I don't know. Maybe. Sometimes. When you're on my mind and making me crazy."

His smile widened. "I still do that?"

"Even excluding our current situation, yes, you do."

"You're going back to that death wish you think I have, aren't you?"

"In a sense. And I don't think, McBride, I know. I can't count the number of times during our marriage that you dragged yourself through the door, bruised and battered and unwilling to tell me why."

"I didn't want to bring the ugly aspect of my work home to you."

"Right, just your bruised and battered body. Where's the problem in that? I should just ignore it, and your black hole of a mood, and go out for dinner with you. Because food eaten in a noisy bistro where conversation is virtually impossible is the answer to all our communication problems. And life rolls on. Until the day you don't come home all messed up and moody, because you just plain don't come home at all, and the next time I see you, you're lying on a slab in the morgue, and I have no idea why." On a roll, she tapped another email open and made an irritated sound. "I hate it when people do that."

"What? Don't come home or end up in the morgue?"

Although she was tempted to hiss at him—and herself as well for venting so much without any real provocation—she merely took a deep breath. "YAMAN wants to be my Facebook friend."

"Sounds Jamaican."

Okay, that was worth a smothered laugh.

"Is there a message?" he asked.

"YAMAN says we share a common bond, a powerful one. He—or she—wants to know if I'm intrigued enough to learn more, dot, dot, dot."

"Are you?"

"Not right now… Oh… Hmm." She cocked her head. "He sent me another message." A slithery sensation crawled through her. "Why does that creep me out?"

"Because it makes him seem like a stalker."

"Unless it's a woman, which takes us back to— Whoa!" She reared back. "This is not good."

He shot her a sideways look. "What?"

"A bad joke, I hope. Really hope. It says, You're ignoring me, Dr. Norris. That's not how the game is played. The loss I suffered because of you will not go unpunished. You'll pay in kind. A death for a death. Be forewarned. YAMAN."

Fear prickled her skin as she rescanned the text. "Be forewarned," she repeated, then felt her blood turn to ice. "Crap, McBride. The second message was sent yesterday afternoon." She met his eyes. "Before the shoot-out at the motel."

McBride had a hard time believing that anyone would want to hurt Alessandra, let alone kill her. But a death for a death? Predicted hours before a three-way shoot-out at a small town motel? A shoot-out that shouldn't have gone down the way it had. No matter how he re-worked the bottom line, Casey Simms had sent her fa-vorite sniper after McBride, and she wasn't one to waste either money or manpower. The rifle guy was unlikely to have been dispatched by her.

On the flipside, coincidences happened, more often than people thought. A hotheaded breeder who'd lost a prize bull might be angry enough and stupid enough to take that step into the abyss, especially after his attempt to ambush the person he deemed responsible for the loss had been thwarted. Add in copious amounts of alcohol, which Alessandra said the man was known to imbibe, and you had nitro walking. But coming after Alessandra with an assault rifle?

No matter how many times he ran it, that scenario didn't play, either. The threat part, possibly. The rifle attack, no.

Although it took her the better part of an hour to get there, Alessandra finally came around. Sort of.

"All right." She folded her arms across her chest, a defiant gesture he recognized well. "Let's go strictly with the facts for now. Any way you look at it, the time aspect is freaky. YAMAN's second email was sent early in the afternoon. Rifle shots were fired at night. Those shots were fired with Eddie there and firing, too."

McBride slowed Moe's black truck as they ap-proached the town of Loden, Wyoming, population six hundred and eighty-eight. A sign on the sparsely treed outskirts proclaimed the one hundred and seventy-fifth anniversary celebration was in full swing. It would be a week of parades, fireworks, entertainment and barbecues. Main Street would be closed to traffic during the event, and a temporary visitors' bureau had been set up in the sheriff's office.

He followed the hand-painted detour signs. "I'm no expert, Alessandra, but I might be able to trace those emails."

She regarded him through her lashes. "At the risk of sounding pessimistic, I thought you had trust issues with the people in your office."

He grinned. "What, you think I haven't picked up any skills over the years?"

"I can envision several, but I wouldn't have put computer hacking among them." She watched a pickup filled with wooden crates behind them via the side mirror. "Larry said Eddie was killed by a rifle bullet."

"What's your point?"

"Nothing. It was just a statement. And, I admit, a niggle that won't go away. Part of me thinks YAMAN could be Frank Hawley. He's obsessive about his livestock and his bulls in particular. He has a vicious temper. He also has a son-in-law named Ryder." She stuck her sunglasses on top of her head and unplugged her Black-Berry from the lighter to check the charge. "Ryder used to be in the military. Now he works with Hawley."

"Breeding bulls?"

"Training horses. On his own ranch, which is adjacent to his father-in-law's. But they're tight, and Ryder loves to drink and fight."

"To excess?"

"I suppose that would depend on your definition." She waited a beat, then added, "He's come on to me more than once since I started working at the clinic."

McBride understood and accepted the jealous gremlin

that sank its claws into his heart, but the suspicion had no real place in his former-cop mind. In spite of that, he narrowed his eyes. "What exactly did 'coming on to you' entail?"

"Pretty much what you'd think—nice dinner, decent club, lots of drinking, hot sex."

Something dark and unpleasant churned in McBride's belly. "You had hot sex with a married man?"

Her lips moved into an ingenuous smile. "Are you asking as Marshal McBride or the man from whom I'm legally separated?"

"I'm trying to remain impartial as both. Why don't we go back to 'Ryder loves to drink and fight,' and see where that takes us."

"I didn't do any of those things with him, McBride. All I said was that he asked me. And—okay, not married—but you came on to me once or twice yourself, you know."

Now the look he slanted her had a wry edge. "You're not going to let this go, are you?"

"Come to think of it, so did the bus driver."

"The bus-crash driver? You never told me that."

Amusement flitted across her face. "He was a jerk, and I was just one of several females he tried to move on. My turn came at the first rest stop. The woman sitting across from me at the beginning of the trip—the one who wound up with a broken leg and a concussion—was number two. The blonde from Arizona came in at number three. And right before we went into the skid, I saw him talking to a sheet welder named Georgia."

Her gaze got distracted by a swooping, soaring hawk in the distance. "I heard Georgia died a month or so after the crash. The blonde didn't make it out of the bus."

"I saw the blonde. Impaled by a piece of glass. How did Georgia die?"

"Not sure. I only know her death was unrelated to the accident. All I really wanted to do was shove the entire thing to the back of my mind and get on with living."

Even more so after she'd watched her seatmate die from massive internal injuries.

"You know," she mused, still tracking the hawk, "the irony is there's not one part of that trip I can't recall with vivid clarity. The before and a lot of the after is fuzzy, but that long string of hours never fades. The roll went on forever. So did the screaming. I can smell the fuel, see electrical wires sparking, hear people crying. There was so much blood, and God, I was so scared."

She'd handled it, though, McBride recalled. She'd gone deep, patched the cracks and dealt with the aftermath.

"I wasn't supposed to be sitting so far back," she continued. "And suddenly, after the roll, there was no way forward. The guy beside me was pinned under an overhead compartment that tore loose and I knew, somehow, that no matter how quickly help arrived, he wasn't going to live. Maybe neither of us were. It was..." She paused, frowned, then let out a deep whoosh of breath. "Wow. I really went off on a tangent there, didn't I? From 'the driver came on to me' to the part, or almost to the part, where I saw your face for the first time." She rested her head on the seat back. "My mother would have called our meeting fate. My father called it a judgment. Not the harshest one in my case, because, while I wasn't the most obedient daughter, I wasn't a really bad one, either."

"By your father's measure, only the bad die young."

She dropped her dark glasses back in place as he

rounded a bend and the last rays of daylight streamed through the windshield. "If his measure had any merit, McBride, you'd have been dead long before we met. I'm glad you weren't and we did meet, but we've strayed miles from our original topic."

Which was—and he had to think hard because he'd had as many nightmares about that crash as she had—whether a horse trainer named Ryder might have been bribed, talked or manipulated into avenging his father-in-law's grievance. And that was understating the matter.

"I don't think Ryder would go that far," Alessandra remarked, eerily reading his mind. "I'm not even sure I think Hawley would." She leaned forward to peer through the windshield. "Is that a cop?"

"Squad car gave it away, huh?"

She grinned. "You're so busted, McBride."

"For what? Driving a borrowed truck?"

"Doing thirty-five in a fifteen-mile-an-hour zone."

"For a small-town girl, that's a bitter stereotype."

"You never met my childhood sheriff. By-the-Book was his first, middle and last name."

In this case, it wasn't the sheriff who pulled them over, but a rail-thin deputy named Barney Pepper. He sniffed as he stuck an envelope and a jar of honey through McBride's rolled-down window. "Welcome to Loden and the one hundred and seventy-fifth anniversary of our town's founding. Honey's local. Hotel's full. Lakeside and mountain cabins are mostly empty on account of Hank Tupper's a mean old cuss who hates people, especially strangers, so he charges sky-high prices hoping folks'll just move along and leave him be. Still, if you don't mind getting hosed, he'll probably accommodate you, seeing as he likes to drink and gamble and he can't do those things for free. Enjoy your stay." With an attempt at a smile, the deputy touched his cap and stepped back.

Amusement swam into Alessandra's eyes. When McBride pulled away, she glanced back at the man, then down at the honey in her hand. "Just imagine all the people, places and events I'd have missed if we'd never met. Hit men, fugitives, Larry, Curly, Moe, Three-Fingers Morley, a cook who swings a mean spatula and now Deputy Barney Fife, handing out jars of Aunt Bea's honey, except here, they spell it B-E-E." Leaning across the seat, she kissed his cheek. "He calls it Loden, but I say welcome to Mayberry."

Emotions he'd been struggling to lock down coiled and thrashed in McBride's belly. But it was the kiss, that soft brush of her lips across his skin, that did it.

With the deputy out of sight, he whipped the truck onto the shoulder, hit the brakes and, before she could sit back, snared her wrist. "Not so fast, darlin'. First up, this isn't Mayberry, or anywhere close to it. Second, people, places and events aside, I never meant to put your life in danger. And third, I've been waiting to do this since I saw you in that parking lot Friday night."

"McBride, don't." She set a warning palm on his chest.

Ignoring the protest, he drew her forward. "Welcome back to my life, Alessandra. And everything that comes with it."

He gave her two seconds to pull free, then hauled her across the console and crushed his mouth onto hers.

HEAT AND HUNGER swirled up so swiftly that the denial, partly formed in Alessandra's throat, emerged as nothing more than a moan of pleasure.

His tongue plunged into her mouth, and made her blood sizzle. No one could throw a kiss into sexual overdrive like McBride.

Images of the two of them skin-to-skin, exploring and rediscovering each other's bodies, streaked through her mind. But they were in a truck on the side of a road with a deputy less than half a mile away. She knew it, and she still wanted to strip away McBride's shirt and his jeans. Worse, she wanted him to tear off her clothes so she could straddle him.

All that pent-up desire unleashed from a single mind-blowing kiss that got more and more potent the longer it went on. Part of her was stunned.

She should end it before her sanity dissolved. But his hands were cupping her face, the back of her neck, holding her in place so he could ravish—yes, actually ravish—every inch of her mouth. And she was loving it.

Instead of going with wisdom, she bunched his hair in her fists and matched him stroke for delicious stroke with her tongue. There was a certain smoky darkness, an element of danger in the way he touched her. It hinted at some never quite spoken vice she'd been warned by her father not to want or accept. And never, ever to enjoy.

The memory of that warning had her lips curving as McBride shifted his mouth to her neck, and his hands to her breasts.

Even through her bra and T-shirt, his thumbs on her nipples made her purr. Her eyes opened briefly, and she realized with a choked laugh that she was, in fact, straddling him. God, the things that happened when McBride blindsided her.

It wasn't wanting him to stop so much as the sound of

a vehicle approaching from behind that had her planting her hands on his ribs and pushing herself away.

"Someone's coming," she said, with more reluctance than was probably wise. "We need to keep moving."

"Plan to," he returned, and dropped his mouth on hers for another heart-stopping kiss.

He took her under again, into that lovely forbidden place where common sense evaporated and sensation ruled.

Tiny jitters like bursts of electricity raced along her nerve ends. She remembered everything about him so well, as if no time had passed since the last night they'd made love. The taste of him that was all McBride, the smell of his skin, the feel of his hands on her breasts, her hips, her thighs, her—

Whoa! Like a whip snapping in her brain, Alessandra dragged her mouth free and caught his wrists. "Are you crazy?" With her hands firmly engaged, she tossed her hair back to see. "We're in the middle of nowhere."

His storm-dark gaze fastened on hers. "The location supports my action more than your objection, Alessandra."

She spied a 4x4 coming up behind them and slid down to his level. "Pretty sure it doesn't since the middle of this particular nowhere leads directly into town. We can't make out in this truck, McBride."

A light of challenge burned in his eyes. "Wanna bet?"

"No... Yes... No!" She squeezed his wrists and tried to wriggle free. When he smiled, she twisted just enough to threaten him with her knee. "Okay, I know you could get out of this all too easily, but I'm trying to convey a message about time, place and the fact that we're separated for a reason."

"One that has nothing to do with sex."

"Truck, road, town," she reminded him for lack of a better comeback.

His eyes traveled to her navel and the jeans he'd managed to unzip. "Sex was never the problem for us. But I don't suppose it's the answer, either."

"Just a fun trip." Sidestepping regret, she worked the zipper up and climbed off him.

She was doing up the buttons and willing her heart back to a seminormal rhythm when she heard the sounds—two echoing gunshots, fired from a point directly ahead.

Chapter Ten

Alessandra knew he took her with him because to leave her alone in the truck would have been even more risky. But while these were gun and not rifle shots, the weapon sounded powerful, and the third one sent a shower of bark flying in all directions.

McBride pulled her to a halt, then into a crouch behind a tall pine.

"Is it Rory?" She squinted over his shoulder.

"Not unless he's decided to wear a fake beard—" another bullet whizzed past "—lost six inches and dropped eighty pounds. Could be last night's rifle guy, though."

Alessandra ducked as two more shots lodged in the trunk. "If it means anything, Ryder—Hawley's son-in-law—doesn't have a beard, he's over six feet tall and he's built like a heavyweight boxer. Hawley's a bit shorter and looks like a bulldog."

"Good to know." McBride nudged her back. "Stay down."

She pointed toward a swaying thicket. "Someone's in there."

He nodded, aimed his gun skyward. "Can you keep him busy while I circle?"

"I'll do my best."

Even as she said it, her heart hammered, her eyes

stung and her palms went damp. But she steeled herself and fired shots around the thicket at intervals she hoped would allow McBride sufficient time to work his way through the underbrush and ambush the shooter. She was waiting out a fresh flurry of bullets and starting to worry about how many of her own she had left when she heard a sharp crack of branches breaking. A loud "Oomph" and a great deal of muffled swearing followed.

Releasing the trigger, Alessandra offered a cautious, "McBride?"

"Back here," he called above the curses. "I've got the shooter and his gun."

It didn't take her long to find him—and the slight man with the mangy red beard who was his prisoner.

Bare-chested and wearing a pair of torn overalls, he looked like a cross between a biker and a cartoon hill-billy. Every inch of exposed skin below his chin was covered with tattoos. His feet, also bare, were the same color as the dirt, and she seriously doubted he'd used a toothbrush in the past decade.

McBride was crouched several feet away. His captive had pushed himself to a sitting position, and was currently scowling at the ground.

"You got no right." He glared at McBride, then at her. "You can't just... Woo-hoo." He cut himself off, blinked, gaped. "You *are* a looker, aren't you?"

"Interesting inflection," McBride remarked. "Gives me the impression someone's described her to you."

The man's mouth clamped shut, and he returned his eyes to the ground. "I'm not saying another word."

"No problem. We'll just take this to the sheriff and see what he makes of it."

"I was shooting squirrels," the man maintained. "Nothing to prove I wasn't."

McBride grinned. "Nothing at all, Billy. It's our word against yours."

"That's right." The man spit into the weeds. "Even a toad with a badge can't say different unless he's got a wit—" He stopped midword but didn't close his mouth. Only his eyes moved back and forth between them. "How'd you—er, what'd you call me?"

McBride snapped a fresh clip into his gun, offered a lethal smile. "Word is you and Rory go way back, to a time when he was looking to break away from the family and set up a little out of country business of his own. Didn't happen, and Rory slunk home with his tail between his legs a whole lot poorer after all the payoffs had been quietly dealt with. But the important thing was, his family never really knew what went down during that fourteen-month stretch of time, or who it went down with."

Billy's tongue flicked out to moisten his lips. His eyes under bushy brows turned to slits. "Don't know what you're talking about."

"Oh, I think you do," McBride said with an easy shrug. "But it doesn't matter. Not to me, anyway. Your sheriff might have a different view of things."

His captive blustered up. "All I hear is blah, blah, blah, lawman. And don't ask how I know what you are. Badge is right there on your belt loop. Sheriff here's got no reason to question me. I don't cause trouble, and he doesn't bug me on account of I keep the local riffraff in line because they're all talk, and I can shoot the wings off a gnat at fifty paces."

"Lots of useless information in there. Now tell me where Rory is before I do a little shooting of my own."

"Go ahead," Billy sneered. "If you got the balls."

Alessandra sighed and stepped back. McBride held

the man's gaze and squeezed the trigger. A rock jumped up from between Billy's legs, caught him on the cheek and had him scuttling sideways in startled fear.

"You're crazy," he accused. "Really crazy. You coulda shot my... Man, it's no wonder Ror—" He broke off, wedged himself against a tree trunk. "Crazy." Anger and resentment joined the fear. "I didn't come anywhere near that close with you." He fingered his cheek. "Am I bleeding?"

"A little," Alessandra told him. "Look, Billy, McBride doesn't care about you."

"I can see that."

His baleful glance brought an absurd swell of humor to her throat. "If you tell us where Rory is, it can end right here."

"Is that you saying so, or him?"

"Her." McBride's lips formed a pleasant smile. "Best you can hope for is that the crazy man'll go along with the lady and not turn you into a eunuch." All amusement vanished. "Where Rory, Billy?"

The man's shoulders hunched. "Maybe you should shoot off one of my toes or something so I can prove how loco you are."

"If you say so." McBride took aim, while Billy snatched his feet up under him.

"Yeah, okay, I get it. He's here, but I don't know where. My place for about five minutes before a truck backfired and spooked him. He told me what you were driving and asked could I throw you off the scent if you showed up. Throw you off," he repeated. "Not shoot off body parts or even draw blood. I said sure and scampered on over to the detour route. Saw you stopped, and figured I might as well go for it."

Alessandra nudged Billy's dropped gun in McBride's

direction. "You do know there's a deputy just down the road."

The man snickered. "Yeah, good old Barn's a real worry. He's so useless, he helped a thief get away from Ike's corner store one night. There's old Ike shouting and Barney boy telling him to zip it and holding the door for the thief's lady friend. Luckier for you than me, he didn't come barreling in to help. There was this other time, too—"

"Rory," McBride interrupted.

"Hey, I was just—"

"Stalling."

"I don't know where he is," the man repeated.

"Yeah, we got that part. Tell us where he might be."

Billy shrugged a shoulder. "Bar, maybe. It's getting late, and he probably figured I'd be able to do the pied piper thing and lead you away from town like he wanted, so he... What?" He scowled when McBride motioned him to his feet. "You think I'm gonna march you around until you nab him?"

"We can start there," McBride agreed. "If that doesn't work, we'll move on to plan B."

Billy's lip curled. "Would that be the plan where you haul my butt into the sheriff?"

"No, the sheriff's plan C." Keeping his eyes on Billy's face, McBride pointed the gun at the man's bare feet. "Plan B's where I start shooting off toes."

OF COURSE IT WAS a bluff, but while it got Billy moving, Alessandra didn't expect it to work. They might have gotten farther, though, if barefoot Billy hadn't stomped across an unpaved parking lot outside one of the seediest bars Alessandra had ever seen, stepped on a broken wagon bolt and punched a hole the size of a nickel in his sole. The shaft was jagged, over two inches long, and if the head was any indication, rust was its main component.

Billy screamed like a girl while Alessandra worked it back out. When he saw the blood that came with it, he turned green and promptly chugged back half the bottle of bourbon someone from inside the bar shoved in his hand.

"Shoulda had a pair of work boots tattooed on your feet," a middle-aged woman with dyed blond hair and tight red jeans scoffed. When he let out a series of high-pitched squeals, she kicked his hip. "Oh, grow some balls, Billy Joe. My baby girl didn't carry on like you when she had three molars yanked last month and the freezing didn't take."

Billy gave her a horrified look and chugged again.

While the bystanders wandered back inside the poorly lit building, the woman plunked her ample butt on a felled log and lit a brown cigarette that smelled like smoked cherries.

"Ad says they'll help me quit. So far they just make me sick. Name's Barb Winchell. Now you—" she one-eyed Alessandra "—you'd be some kind of doc. And you—" she stabbed her cigarette at McBride "—you're either my fantasy come to life or a cop from someplace hell and gone more interesting than this spit hole of a town. Did you get your honey jar coming in?"

"Aunt Bee's famous," Alessandra confirmed. "This is going to sting," she told Billy, who shrieked before she pulled the antiseptic from the medi-pack.

"You don't do teeth, do you?" Barb asked.

"Only for animals." McBride went to his haunches to watch and have a deceptively affable chat. Or maybe not so deceptive, Alessandra reflected with a glance at the woman's fox-sharp features. "Got any games going inside, Barb?"

She blew a stream of smoke. "Depends who's asking and why."

"I'm looking for a man named Rory Simms. Big, ugly, hands the size of bear paws, diagonal slash across his collarbone."

"Mud-brown hair," Alessandra added. "Acne-scarred face."

"Sounds about average for this place. But since the one you mean'd be a stranger, answer is the same as before. Depends who's asking and why."

At Billy's sour expression, McBride grinned and explained in fifty words or less. Which was approximately forty-five words more than Alessandra had gotten out of him under similar circumstances during their marriage.

"U.S. marshal, huh?" Barb shrugged with her mouth. "That's a new one in these parts. And it doesn't surprise me that Billy here'd be pals with an escaped felon. I can't say as anyone with a diagonal scar's been here, but you could try Luke's place. Luke's my cousin. Real tight-ass. He has a bar in town. South end, two blocks off Main on Hooper Street. I gotta tell you, hon, that man's got more stuff going on than a Las Vegas fun house. I run a few games, but nothing like Luke's. Nothing rigged, but plenty of players every night."

"Rat," Billy slurred. Then his head lolled, his eyes crossed and he toppled from the log onto the gravel lot.

Barb coughed out a laugh. "If the guy you're looking for's half as dumb as this bottle of charged water, you won't have any trouble rounding him up at Luke's."

"He's not quite as dumb." McBride stood. "But he's plenty predictable."

"He's also desperate." Alessandra repacked the medical kit, snapped the lock and gave Billy's leg a pat. "We're also thinking he might be out of money."

Which really only left one question in her mind. But it was a big one, and no matter how hard she tried to set it aside, she couldn't. Rory had told her that, despite a fabricated reputation, he was terrible with firearms. If that was true, then who'd been using the assault rifle that had killed Eddie Rickard?

WHILE SHE MIGHT not be able to banish the question completely, it wasn't difficult for Alessandra to banish it from the forefront of her mind.

If possible, Luke's Bar was even more of a dive than his cousin Barb's. Leaving a rather boisterous street celebration behind them, McBride pushed through a poorly hung door into a low-lit room that smelled like whiskey, sweat and cigarettes. Dead center of the room stood a fighting cage. It had a concave canvas floor and more dark streaks and splotches than Alessandra could count.

Lovely, she thought, and tugged the hat he'd placed on her head a little lower.

Deep inside, she spied three pool tables. The clack of balls rose above stuttering Amy Winehouse. Someone whacked the jukebox, and the stutter stopped.

She felt as if hidden eyes locked on and tracked them as they made their way across the floor. Nothing obvious, but the sensation of ants on her skin escalated with every step.

"I should have closed the clinic before Smith and his dog rolled up Friday night," she murmured, taking a covert look around. "Then I would have never gotten mixed up with this...and you."

"That'll learn ya, darlin'." There was a faint tease in

McBride's tone, but she noticed his eyes never stopped moving. And he kept a firm hold on her hand.

She bumped his shoulder. "Tell me again why we didn't ask the sheriff for help."

"Too many cooks, Alessandra."

"Yes, you said that before. It's not an answer."

"I called his office while you were pulling that spike out of Billy's foot. Sheriff's in Cheyenne for a few days. Family emergency. You met Deputy Pepper. His counterpart didn't inspire a whole lot more confidence, and I'm not big on official clutter in any case."

"I really should have closed the clinic on time."

He'd insisted she wear a jacket, so it only took a few minutes for the heat to set on edge what few nerves she was managing to keep under control.

"He's not playing pool," she noted, as she looked around the bar. "Any sign of a back room?"

"Not so far." He sounded preoccupied so she followed his gaze and tried to guess why he was staring at the kitchen.

A man's voice cut in before she could ask.

"You looking for me?"

McBride's eyes remained on the kitchen as he replied, "If you're Luke, yeah."

They turned to regard a man half as large as Rory. When he and McBride moved aside, Alessandra gave him a long good look.

Barb's cousin was short, ripped and openly defiant. He made her think of a wolverine and not the *X-Men* kind. She sensed a strong bite-first-ask-any-serious-questions-later attitude. In other words, nothing McBride couldn't handle.

Swinging around, she made a more thorough study of the room.

"You ever been in the cage?" someone behind her asked.

She glanced back at a woman with shorn black hair, black shorts and large, rippling biceps. "Not really my thing." She regarded the dark streaks on the floor. "It looks...painful."

"Can be if you're slow and stupid. I smell class and Ralph Lauren perfume under that flyboy jacket you're wearing. What is it you're hoping to find in here? Lie and say a job and I'll pop you in the mouth."

Alessandra believed her. "My, uh, husband's looking for someone. A man."

"We got a lot of those."

"This one's big, he's bad and he has a scar on his collarbone."

"What's his sin?"

"He's an escaped felon. A murderer."

"His vice?"

"Gambling and women."

"Double whammy. Clover!" She shouted above hoots, pool balls and Rascal Flatts at maximum volume.

The woman who wandered over had ice-blue eyes set in a sun-weathered forty-something face.

"Big, ugly, with a scar here." Alessandra's companion used a skull-painted fingertip to demonstrate. "Seen him anywhere?"

Clover's smile was slow and sly. "Sounds like the guy who got lucky at craps a while back. He gave Sue fifty bucks to send anyone with questions on to Elbow— that's a town fifty miles north of here." The blue eyes twinkled. "Too bad for him Sue's shift ended five minutes later. Badder still he didn't give me the fifty."

Recognizing the game, Alessandra tilted her head

at a speculative angle. "I can do a hundred—fifty a piece—if you tell me where he is now."

"She's with a cop," the first woman warned the one named Clover. "Helluva looker, but still a cop. He's talking to Luke, who doesn't look happy."

"Luke never looks happy." Clover sashayed closer. "Fifty more, pretty sister, and we'll waylay the boss while you and the cop check out the door down the hall. If your guy's still there and you see Margo, tell her we said hi."

She'd probably regret this, Alessandra thought, but slipped her hand into McBride's pocket, located his wallet and hoped he had sufficient cash.

He did. Five seconds after it disappeared into a pair of bras, the women went flying over a table and came up scratching, clawing and kicking.

A potbellied man elbowed past. "I got twenty on Clover."

"Fifty on Raven," someone else shouted.

And the stampede began. Men who'd been leering moments before now jostled and bumped her aside. Luke jumped into the fray, and even the cooks rushed out of the kitchen.

She was watching money change hands at a fast and furious rate when McBride grabbed her. "You might not like my world, Alessandra, but you're finding your niche fast enough. I almost didn't feel you picking my pocket."

He'd set his mouth close to her ear, so close a shiver of something—excitement?—shimmered through her bloodstream.

Exasperated with herself, she turned her head, stared for a moment, then kissed him. Long and hard and with just enough mad around the edges to make a statement.

When she pulled free, her whole mouth tingled. Served her right for attempting to prove a nonexistent point.

"I'm going insane," she decided. "If it isn't all about sex, and it shouldn't be in any healthy relationship, why can't I stop thinking about it and you at all the wrong moments?"

"Because sex and danger go hand in hand, and we've been immersed in the second thing since Friday night."

Her lips tipped into a false smile. "Well, I feel better. But before we abandon reason and start making out on the floor, you should know that Rory might be doing exactly that in a hidden room down a hallway next to the kitchen. The info plus diversion cost you a hundred and fifty bucks, but I'm betting it's accurate. Call's yours, McBride. If we go in, though, I'm staying behind you. A naked Rory Simms isn't something I want to see right now."

"Don't blame you." With a quick kiss—for luck, he claimed—McBride took her hand and forged a path through the sea of cheering bodies to a barely visible opening at the far end of the bar.

A pool ball had jumped off one of the tables and rolled between her feet. Alessandra picked it up while McBride pulled out his Glock.

Sex, danger and a sleek powerful weapon in the right hands. The thrill had to be in the mix. Toss in McBride himself, and the heat factor shot off the scale.

The jukebox played on. The women fought on. Halfway down the narrow corridor, McBride held her back with a hand, listened at a door, then tried the knob. When the latch held, he backed up a step and gave it a kick.

It had to be bad luck that Rory's back was to the window and the woman in front of him, who hastily grabbed a sheet, blocked any shot McBride might have had. Openmouthed and obviously startled, Rory snatched up the pants that were puddled at his feet and dove across the sill.

The woman dropped the sheet and streaked to the opening. Red-faced and determined, she started to climb out herself, swearing and flailing at McBride behind her.

Unable to think of anything better, Alessandra rushed over and grabbed her hair. The woman whirled, a light of fury glowing in her black-rimmed eyes.

"Go." She waved McBride forward. "I can handle this." She hoped.

Huffing like an enraged bull, the woman gave her a shove, then stomped around the room searching for her clothes. "You had no right to barge in," she shouted, and banged a fist on the wall for effect. "That's half my rent money that just jumped out the window. He's the first guy who's shown any interest in ten days, and you make him cut out without paying. I'm sick of the cage. Raven's faster than me, and younger. One day, I'm gonna get killed on that canvas." Her mouth took an unappealing downward turn. "Who are you, anyway?"

Keeping her distance, Alessandra threw a bright green tank top across the bed. "It's a very long, very complicated story. But believe me when I tell you, you're better off wrestling Raven than Rory."

"Bull. You ever fought Raven?"

"No. Have you ever fought a murderer?"

"Yes." The woman's sneer gave way to a fierce and frightening smile. Using her top like a rope, she snapped the fabric. "Know what else?" She bent forward to offer a menacing, "I won."

Chapter Eleven

Rory plunged into the heart of the street party. And he was smart enough to run hunched over so McBride couldn't see his head. Still, his path of destruction was wide, and more than one disgruntled bystander aimed a boot at him.

"That way," a grandfather with a corn dog told McBride. "Could be he's going for the old livery. Fella gets in there, even one the size of a moose, you'll have a devil of a time fishing him out."

A voice in McBride's head nagged him as he worked through the crowd in the direction of the distant livery. It echoed and got louder with every step. *It's not as simple as it appears.... There's something more to this, something obscured by the obvious....*

He spotted his quarry fifty yards ahead. Rory was going for the big barn all right. Made sense. Spillage from the anniversary celebration littered the mouth of the building. There were wagons and flatbeds, tractors, trucks and trailers. Parade floats had been stripped down and others were under construction. Arches and canopies, ramps and rigging were stacked, strewn or leaning on every available surface.

McBride used the larger vehicles for cover in case Rory decided to shoot. That he didn't suggested he'd placed unwarranted faith in his Loden contact and possibly in the late Eddie Rickard.

As the din from the festival receded, McBride picked up the closer sounds of rushing feet, heard an unwieldy body crashing into assorted protrusions. He gave his eyes five seconds to adjust, then eased across the threshold and into the shadows.

Like him, Rory opted to stop. Question was, where in this jam-packed welter of parade paraphernalia would a frantic fugitive feel it was safe to slide in and sweat it out?

Gun up, McBride skirted the rows of stacked crates that, in his opinion, represented the best hiding spots. He checked under wagons and inside an old Pullman on street wheels. The worn velvet seats contained nothing but dust. The shades were up and none of the shadows around them stirred.

He was ten feet past the train car when he heard a small scrape. "Gotcha, Rory," he said softly, and, bringing his gun down, fired in the direction of the sound.

As he'd hoped, Rory surged up from behind a gray surrey, froze like a bloated ferret, then bolted.

He lumbered toward the back of the building. Since there was no door visible, McBride figured he'd switch directions the moment he spotted decent cover and try for the side exit. Jamming his gun into his waistband, he vaulted over a pair of sawhorses, followed a long shadow and arrived there at the same time.

Rory barreled into sight, saw him and braked. "I told her to tell you to back off," he shouted.

He launched a box of metal parts at McBride's head. Finally, he pulled out a gun. He squeezed off two shots, plus an over-the-shoulder third. McBride considered firing back, but figured he was close enough to go for the tackle.

They'd been positioned at right angles to each other. A dozen running steps, a hop up onto the tongue of a wooden wagon and he had Rory knocked down and bucking on the packed dirt floor.

The impact, struggle and brief exchange of punches produced more than a little blood and, in McBride's case, a pain that seared from shoulder to wrist. Still, the damage was lighter than it could have been.

"You think this is over, McBride, but it's not. Eddie'll see to that. When he catches—"

"Eddie's dead, Rory."

"What?" The big man's head reared up. "You killed him?"

"Someone did. A bullet caught him between the ribs. He bled to death in his truck last night."

"But…" The fight simply drained out of him. "Eddie's dead?"

McBride swiped an arm across his face, came up with a smear of blood and grimaced. "I thought you told Alessandra you didn't care if he died."

"I don't… I did. But it wasn't supposed to go like this. Him dead and me caught. Casey'll kill you now for sure." His brow furrowed, "Me, too, maybe. Hell!"

It was the terror in the last word that had McBride bracing to offset the mighty heave that almost pitched him from Rory's back. He managed to get his forearm across his prisoner's neck. "I'm willing to bet the rifle used on Alessandra and me a few nights ago is the one responsible for Eddie's death. Assuming your sister didn't dispatch another henchman, that only leaves one viable suspect as triggerman. You were in the vicinity, Rory, and I don't think you trust your sister to keep you alive any more than she trusts you to keep the family's secrets."

A powerful shudder passed through Rory's body. The single eye he turned in McBride's direction glinted, but whether from fear or derision he couldn't be sure.

"You find that rifle," Rory told him in a flat, emotionless tone. "But you better do it fast because whatever Casey has planned for me, she'll plan it double for you, and, yeah, your pretty lady friend, too. I'm telling you, and I ain't lying. The only time I ever picked up a rifle was when I was fifteen years old and my best buddy's grandpa left his old Varminter lying loose in the basement. I pulled the trigger once and blew my buddy's arm off at the elbow. I haven't touched another one since." His eye—still unreadable—glinted again. "Choice is yours, McBride. Are you gonna take the word of a murderer, or take your chances with the murderer's untrustworthy sister?"

THE SYSTEM OF PROCESSING criminals in Loden required a stream of back and forth phone calls, misplaced arrest forms and, all tolled, approximately two more hours of patience than McBride currently possessed.

By midnight, the out of town sheriff told McBride to ignore his bickering deputies and work with the dispatcher to arrange transportation of the prisoner to a holding cell in Cheyenne.

In the end, and with a headache the size of the Grand Tetons slamming in his skull, McBride decided to do the transporting himself. A local rancher volunteered to ride shotgun. That was Rory taken care of.

But no way was McBride taking Alessandra to Cheyenne. Not with a live bomb on board. Against his better judgment, he let her talk him into leaving her in Loden for the day, thanked the hotel manager for the space that miraculously opened up and finally hauled his gear into the rustic lobby.

"You're in the honeymoon suite," the woman at the desk informed him. She grinned and winked. "I sent your pretty lady up ten minutes ago. Told her we'd get the rest of her things to her as soon as Marvin's finished with the fireworks display."

"Ten minutes?" McBride looked up from the register Alessandra had already signed. "She's been here for ninety."

"I know, but we got to talking. One thing led to another, and my cat's been feeling poorly lately, so she offered to take a look at him. He's eighteen, and it turns out his thyroid's probably out of whack, like his mama's." She winked again. "Dr. Norris says that's a fixable feline problem, so to show my gratitude, I sent a bottle of red wine to your room, because red's romantic, and the two of you look so damn good together, I couldn't resist. Now don't you worry about those bags. They'll be sitting outside your door next time you open it."

Feeling achy and tired, McBride made the most expedient exit he could—unfortunately, not fast enough to avoid the two dozen Facebook photos of her grandchildren. Finally, he climbed the narrow staircases to the third floor.

He expected Alessandra either to be asleep on the bed or soaking in a hot tub, if there was a tub, he thought. But all he could see when he opened the door was her mile-long legs crossed and propped up on the windowsill. She wore her calf-high suede boots, his battered leather jacket and hat, a pair of really skimpy lace panties and, if his suddenly empty brain wasn't hallucinating, absolutely nothing else.

"'Bout time you showed up, Marshal." Her amused drawl made his throat go dry. Without looking over, she dangled a glass of ruby-red claret. "I gotta tell you, this wine is good. Damn good. The desk lady really knows her California labels." Head provocatively angled, she cast him a sultry look from under her lashes. "You want it, honey lamb, you're gonna have to come and get it."

Okay, he could either go with this—and God knew he wanted to—or he could take the high road, which God also knew had never been his way. Booting the door shut, he started toward her. "Are you drunk?"

She smiled. "Maybe. A little. Do you care?"

"I always care, Alessandra."

"I'll rephrase, then. Does it matter?"

"Same answer, darlin', but with a lot more restraint." His gaze dropped to the shadowy swell of her breasts and didn't want to leave. He forced the issue and met her stunning eyes, eyes made even a deeper shade of gold by the lamplight glowing in the corner of the room. "Why the seduction scene?"

She laughed, and the sound of it sent a surge of blood straight to his groin.

"Because it's over, McBride. But before it ended and the danger level reached its peak, it occurred to me that life is very short." Her booted feet hit the floor. "And you, Marshal McBride, are very hot." She stood in a single liquid motion that put a glitch in but didn't halt his inexorable advance. "You're also the man to whom I said 'for better or worse.' I'll admit, I went through more of the second thing than the first for the bulk of our marriage, but as you pointed out, I knew what I was getting into when I said 'I do' to a cop. So maybe the split was no one's fault." Close enough now that he could feel the warmth of her skin, she hooked her arms around his neck and stared into his still-shielded eyes. "I really have to say it again. You truly are one überhot lawman. Even if sex isn't everything in a relationship, ours was always top-notch, and I'm in the mood for a fun and exciting side trip."

Gonna get problematic, McBride reflected inasmuch as he could think with his brain already enveloped in a dark and delicious mist that gave all the power to her and his own churning lust.

He sucked in a breath through his teeth when her hand closed around him and squeezed. "Jesus, Alessandra. Shouldn't we be...?"

Wait. What the hell was he doing? he suddenly wondered. A hot woman—his wife and the woman he loved—wanted hot sex, and he was thinking about objections and stall tactics and having some form of inane conversation with her first?

When he heard the chuckle deep in her throat, he yanked her against him. "You want this, right? You're sure?"

Her eyes sparkled. "A man of few words is my Mc-Bride."

He figured he'd been lucky to get that much out. "I'll call that a yes," he said. Lowering his head, he took possession of her mouth.

And seriously hoped the nagging voice he'd heard earlier had been wrong, even if only for tonight.

ALESSANDRA SUSPECTED she'd been gearing up for this moment since he'd reappeared in her life. Tonight, after everything that had gone down in Luke's Bar, then watching McBride deal with the aftermath of Rory

Simms's arrest in the sheriff's office, she'd been stoked and ready. How could she not love such an unpretentiously sexy, take-charge kind of man?

The more she'd seen, the more she'd wanted, and now, finally, she intended to have.

It wouldn't change anything between them, wouldn't erase or even address the problems that had driven them apart, but for one incredible moment, she'd be able to go back and experience the rush that was McBride.

She didn't want him to be sweet or tentative or particularly gentle. Not that any of those things were McBride's style. Like her, he preferred—well, jungle sex, she supposed. Too bad the hotel didn't provide its guests with animal-print sheets.

Leopard spots began to dance in her head. Then McBride dragged her up onto her toes, covered her mouth with his and blotted out every one of those spots.

He swept her under, down to a lovely, dark world that was all about sensation, with a speed and thoroughness that upped the heat factor substantially and had need galloping like a thoroughbred in her chest.

She'd intended to seduce and entice, to disarm. To do what he might not expect. She'd never meant to let greed swallow her.

But that's what it did. It took her in whole and gave her no time to rethink. Or think at all. The heat and hunger that slammed together left her breathless. And wanting much, much more.

He gripped her hips, pulled his mouth from hers just long enough for his lips to crook up into a faint smile.

Oh, yeah, so McBride.

One easy boost, and her feet left the floor. Her legs curled tightly around him. His arousal burned through the lace of her bikinis and made her breath hitch. One arm at a time, the leather jacket fell away, landing with a soft thud at his feet.

He feasted on her mouth, then sent a shiver of delight along her nerve endings when he lifted her higher to capture one of her breasts.

It was all about waves then, dark billowing swells that rose and fell and rose again. Up and up, until her muscles simply gave out and her head fell back.

He drew her nipple into his mouth, used his teeth and tongue on the tip. Sensation rocked her, hard and fierce. A muffled cry slipped out. Pleasure surged until the need spiking through her won out.

She was desperate for more of him, for all of him. When his mouth shifted back to hers, she untangled her legs and hopped down to tug on his shirt, his jeans, anything and everything that prevented her from getting her hands on him.

Don't stop. Don't slow down. Don't think about the rocky before or the nebulous after. She was on fire, he was hard and they wanted each other. Now.

Crickets and grasshoppers chirped softly outside. An owl hooted. Music of the night, she thought, and breathed in the scent that was a combination of McBride and late summer in a remote mountain town.

The contrast of outright lust and sparkling romance amused her. McBride's head came up. Sort of. When he spoke, it was against her lips and between kisses.

"Just how much wine have you had, Alessandra?"

"Not much." She freed a hand to measure out two inches. Then she caught the ends of his hair in her fists and tugged. "I'm not drunk. I swear. Not on wine, anyway. Not even on the danger aspect." She released his hair, ran her hands along his arms to his ribs and lower, until she heard a hiss of air. "The power, though, and afterward the no-big-deal cop efficiency—" her fingers zeroed in on target "—now those things are really cool."

His eyes, unreadable and dark, swept over her face. "Are you sure about the two inches, darlin'?"

"No." Her lips curved into a teasing smile as her hand closed once again on his erection. "But I'm not going to pass out. I'm also over twenty-one and hungry for something way better than food." With a sultry roll of her hips, she kissed him again. "Mmm, way better than wine, too."

He was holding on to the remnants of his control. She knew it and swore she heard his teeth grinding. Time to go for it. Wrapping a single leg around his hips, she made a slow gyration. She saw his eyes close, heard a sound that might have been a wry laugh and watched the remnants scatter.

Suddenly, both his hands and hers were everywhere, racing over heated skin, digging into taut muscle, sliding through hair and down long limbs.

He backed her across the floor. The bedsprings protested under their weight. The lamp filled the old room with a soft light that was a perfect counterpoint to the fire consuming them from the inside.

Alessandra kissed and nipped at McBride's face—his jaw, his eyelids, his cheekbones. She scraped her fingernails across his shoulders and back. She used her teeth on him, bit his throat and his neck, then gave a gasping laugh when he moved his hand between her legs.

Wires snapped and sizzled and sparked at every pulse point. But when he slid his fingers inside her, the world around them simply vanished.

Her head bowed on the pillow. A thousand frantic little drums beat under her skin. Every part of her throbbed and zinged and pumped. He knew, had always known, how to take her up and over, to bring out the passion inside her.

Her fingers gripped the sheets, her hips arched and the heat, the sparking, sparkling heat, reached staggering proportions.

She hadn't realized she had so much left for him. The shock of that discovery, together with the wonder of her reaction, almost diverted her. But then he angled his body over hers, kissed her senseless and plunged inside.

She didn't know if she cried out—it had been so long, and she'd deliberately locked the passion away—but something, either breath or sound, emerged from her throat. Her heart was a drumbeat, driving her higher. He cuffed her wrists on either side of her head. She saw his eyes, dark and gleaming, his face partly lit by the lamp, his body in silhouette.

Excitement streaked through her veins. It seemed the room was in motion. Or was it her? Or them?

One peak, two. She drew him in again, harder, faster, deeper and at the same time rose to meet him.

Emotions boiled to a climax. She felt the exact moment of his release and matched it with her own. She knew she cried out then, and sank her fingers into his hips for one last glorious burst.

Her skin was hot and damp, her lungs on fire, her brain a delightful blur. He collapsed on top of her, and in spite of the fact that none of her muscles were functioning, she managed a satisfied smile.

She loved it when his self-control disappeared. No more walls, no more hurdles, no more distance, nothing said or unsaid, no charged or hurtful words. Only one beautiful, blissful, disconnected moment in the center of an otherwise stormy marital sea.

Alessandra had no idea how long they lay together while the room and her skin cooled. She felt…happy, she decided, and, letting her lashes fall, steeped her drifting senses in McBride and the night air.

When he eventually stirred, she realized with a trace of amusement that she couldn't breathe, at least not properly. She could, however, feel his heart thudding against hers.

Sliding a foot along his leg, she wiggled. "I think I'm starting to see the tunnel, McBride. With pretty golden angels at the end."

He grunted, used his elbows to lever up. Not far, but enough for her to take in some desperately needed air.

"Lucky lady," he murmured. "All I see is a big orange glow. Guess that tells me where I'm headed." This time when he collapsed, he did so more beside than on top of her. "Not sure, darlin', but it's possible I just had a heart attack."

Humor mingled with delight. Since he was facedown on the mattress now, and not moving, she slid the rest of the way out, climbed on top of him and rested her ear on his back.

"Beat sounds strong and healthy to me, McBride." She ran a hand underneath him. "Feels good, too. Still, I'm no expert…" She drew the words out as her fingers made their way to his groin.

He cut off a breath and rolled onto his back. His hands snagged her waist to hold her in place.

"Oops." She grinned. "Wrong body part."

"Right part, wrong position. Try that again now that we're face-to-face."

Her eyes ran down, then up. "Strong and healthy," she repeated, and let her head dip inch by tantalizing inch, until her mouth almost but not quite touched his.

"What say we try that sex experiment again and see who ends up where—in the fire or the tunnel—and in what condition?"

"It's your funeral, darlin'."

She smiled. "Well, then…" Challenge set, she gave his bottom lip a bite, tightened her fingers around the hard, silky length of him and, holding his eyes with hers, drew him back inside.

Chapter Twelve

Alessandra woke to a roar and the stomach-to-throat sensation of somersaulting down an embankment.

For a disoriented second, she was on a two-lane highway south of Chicago, and forty-six passengers were trying desperately to remain in their seats while tons of bus rolled over a rocky embankment. To her relief, when her surroundings steadied and the shadows settled, there were plank floorboards beneath her and the rumble that was making them shudder came from the sky outside.

Safe, her mind whispered. Releasing a deep breath, she willed her speeding heart to slow down.

Flat on her stomach with the bedsheet tangled around her, she mumbled, "McBride?" When he didn't answer, she sat up. "McBride? Are you here?"

She checked the mattress, realized it was empty and, unwrapping herself from the sheet, got to her knees. Since his backpack was closest, she rummaged inside and found a clean denim shirt. Then her eyes landed on a thermal mug and, dropping the sheet, she knee-walked to the table.

A note beside the mug said, "Taking Rory to Cheyenne. You still sleep like the dead, and look beautiful doing it. Last night—incredible. Wonder who'll have a better day? Love, McBride."

Memories flooded back and made her smile, but it was the coffee that elicited a sigh of pure pleasure. Bless the man for his attention to detail.

A protracted peal of thunder shook the floor again. The bedside clock read 9:22 a.m. The window showed dense black clouds outside and the first fat drops of rain.

In no particular hurry—and, God, wasn't that a treat—Alessandra took her coffee into the bathroom. She showered, then using McBride's shirt as a robe, came out to sit cross-legged on the bed and check her emails.

She'd text Joan and Larry first, eat a really healthy breakfast and, since the street party was bound to be a washout, see what kind of impulse shopping Loden had to offer.

That was the plan, anyway. A fist banging on the door interrupted her before she could compose her first message.

Must be housekeeping, she decided, her attention focused on her BlackBerry. "Not dressed," she called out.

"Got food," Raven countered.

Alessandra glanced at her bare legs. Good enough for another woman. Buttoning the shirt, she got up to let her visitor in.

A stack of something black sat on a plate next to three strips of something even blacker.

"Seriously." Alessandra stared. "What is that?"

"My attempt at waffles and bacon." Raven shoved the otherwise empty tray into her hands. "I'm not much in the kitchen. Unfortunately, Ralph—he's the day cook here—chopped off part of his index finger yesterday afternoon and had to go down to Cheyenne."

Skepticism changed to surprise. "You don't have a doctor in Loden?"

"Hey, we consider ourselves lucky to have a retired army medic. Be better if he wasn't eighty-some years old, but you know the line about beggars. Now, are you gonna be nice and pretend to eat the fruits of my morning's labors, or do I have to toss you in the cage and start my warm-up early?"

Alessandra lifted one of the waffles to see if anything more palatable lurked beneath it. Nothing did. She dusted crumbs from her fingers, offered a polite smile. "Do you have a dog?"

"Yeah, a pit bull named Rip. Why?"

"Tell you what. If Rip'll eat this, then I will, too. If not, I'm off the hook. Fair?"

"Off the breakfast hook, anyway," Raven allowed. "Too bad, though." She strolled to the window. "It's a pisser of a day out there. Win or lose, I could use a little fun with a novice."

Alessandra refrained from covering the tray with a napkin after she set it down. "Such a tempting offer, but…"

She saw it coming, just not soon enough to evade Raven's tattooed arm as it shot out, wrapped itself around her throat. And tightened.

ALESSANDRA WASN'T SURE who was more shocked—her when Raven grabbed her, or Raven when Alessandra snapped her head back and cracked her captor's face. An elbow low, then high, freed her. She dived for her shoulder bag, twisted around and came up with McBride's Sig Sauer pointed at Raven's chest.

"Whoa, whoa, whoa." Palms out, the woman sucked a spot of blood from her split lower lip. "You freeze, I'll freeze. You react fast, lady. I was going for a sleeper, and you got out of it before I had you fully snared."

Alessandra held the gun steady while her heart hammered. "What the hell was that for?"

"It's a grip. I use it in the cage when a fight goes stale." She chuckled at Alessandra's unbelieving expression. "I didn't figure you for the fight-back type, or I'd have put more oomph behind it. It was a demonstration." She rapped her head. "I wanted to see what you were made of. I found out."

Mild irritation moved in. "McBride asked you to watch me, didn't he?"

Raven's slow smile was answer enough. Releasing an exasperated breath, Alessandra let her arms drop and climbed to her feet.

"This is why I left him." She gestured with the gun as she searched for her own pack. "No communication. He sics a watchdog on me, but does he mention it? No. 'Last night was great, darlin'. Here's coffee. Back whenever.'"

"You're really married? How long?"

"Four frustrating years. Five and a half if you include separation time." She located the pack beside a chair and yanked out the clothes she wanted. "You must be what he meant when he said he wondered which one of us would have a better day." Another clap of thunder distracted her attention from her clothes. She looked up at Raven. "Sounds more like dynamite than thunder."

"Storm's a doozy. Listen, can you cook?"

"Yes." Still annoyed, Alessandra rooted through her purse for a hairbrush. "Why?"

"Because obviously I can't. So how about a trade? I'll teach you some more moves, and you can teach me how to bake an edible chocolate fudge cake. It's what I want to bring to the potluck dinner tomorrow night, and so far those waffles over there are closer to the mark than anything I've done in a cake pan. There's nothing else to do, anyway. This weather's gonna get worse before it gets better."

Draping her jeans over one arm, Alessandra started for the bathroom. "Will these moves of yours work on anyone, male or female?"

"Worked on Clover last night. Probably work on a certain marshal tonight." Her mouth quirked up on one side. "If that's what you're asking."

"That's what I'm asking."

"In that case, I hope he likes living on the edge."

Alessandra paused in the doorway, looked back. "Yeah, he does. In fact, I don't think he's ever lived anywhere else."

BY EARLY AFTERNOON, Alessandra pronounced the baking lesson done. And more or less successful. An hour later, the rising storm knocked out power to the south side of Loden. That included both the hotel kitchen and Luke's Bar.

Sick to death of all things food related, Raven coaxed her over to the town's gym/boxing ring, located in a unused storehouse a mile out of town.

Once there, she stuck her iPod in a battery dock, fired up the rusty generator and ordered her pit bull, Rip, who'd refused to eat either her waffles or her bacon, to watch for skunks in the woods. She tossed Alessandra a pair of boxing mitts, but after a quick search through the storage box gave the lid an aggravated slam.

"Crap. Someone swiped the headgear. I'll have to go out to my truck. You can warm up on the ropes until I get back."

Not entirely certain any of this was wise, Alessandra

nevertheless entered the ring. Her phone rang. Hitting Speaker, she began to stretch.

"Not talking to you, McBride," she said with a grunt. "A gentleman would have mentioned that he'd asked someone with biceps of steel to babysit the woman who's going to punch his lights out when he returns to town, which at this moment is functioning on half power and has absolutely nothing happening street-party wise."

He grunted back. "You're still winning the better-day contest, darlin'. A rig jackknifed and puked its load of fresh manure all over the highway. Rory swears the sausage we let him eat at breakfast has given him food poisoning, and I just finished changing a flat with a thirty-mile-an-hour wind blasting rain, mud and gravel in my face."

She took a practice swing, grinned. "You're just trying to make me feel better." Outside, Rip began to bark. She hoped he hadn't spotted a skunk. "Are you in Cheyenne yet?"

"Twenty minutes. Wind's picking up… Could be longer than I thought… Talked to the sheriff…"

Static finished the sentence.

"McBride?" She repositioned her phone several times. "Are you there?" When he didn't respond, she made a face. "You always find a way to weasel out of a conversation, don't you?"

Curling and uncurling her fingers, she listened to the wind howl and Willie Nelson whine. The lights, sparse and already low, flickered. Rip barked again. She thought she heard Raven shout at him.

The door to her left gave a protracted creak, then slammed shut. Whether foolish or not, her heart thumped double time.

With the storm outside, a slamming door, wind in

the rafters and McBride in a dead zone, this was getting creepy. And where was Raven?

Her phone rang again. She didn't look at the caller's name, but answered, "McBride?"

There was nothing, not even static.

With fear beginning to curl in her stomach, she checked the screen. And felt her muscles seize when she saw the name staring back at her.

YAMAN.

Whipping around, she made a quick scan of the storehouse. Nothing moved. She was being paranoid. Maybe. She'd lived with McBride long enough to know that if something felt wrong, it probably was.

Raven should be back. And why was her dog barking? Possibly at skunks. But what if someone had ambushed his owner?

Slipping out of the ring, Alessandra lowered herself, face forward, to the ground. Yes, she could hear the wind, but that didn't mean a more sinister sound lurked beneath. On the other hand, there was YAMAN.

Who was he? Not Rory, or Eddie.

Frank Hawley? His son-in-law, Ryder?

"I didn't kill that bull," she said through her teeth.

Eyes in motion, she picked up McBride's jacket, made another wary circle and started for the door.

Too many shadows, her mind whispered. And the music was much louder now. Raven's playlist had gone from Willie Nelson to full-throttle Steve Tyler.

With her thumb, she speed-dialed McBride's cell. And got no response.

The wind outside made deep swooping sounds. Rain pelted the roof and walls.

Then, sliding in beneath both those noises, she heard a snarl.

Shadows loomed like misshapen monsters between her and the door. The lights fluttered again. The generator coughed.

She could see the person only in silhouette. An instant before the generator stalled, she glimpsed the arm that flew out to hit the switch. And watched as everything went dark.

Stifling a gasp, she ran. But the intruder was closer to the door. He got a hand on her shoulder and wrenched her to a halt.

"Not this time, Doc," he growled. Tossing a blanket over her head, he shoved her into the wall. "One death for another. And another and another and another. Yours, your cop husband's, that bastard...and..."

Thunder rocked the building. He bit out something that sounded like "leopard" as he shoved her into the wall again, and a sea of glittering stars appeared.

Somehow, miraculously, he'd only trapped one of her arms under the blanket. While he continued to shove her, she worked her hand into her jacket pocket and found the pool ball she'd picked up the night before.

His muffled voice filtered through the wool. "There's no one to interfere this time, lady. It's just you and me."

She struck him in the side of the head. She thought she must have connected because his grip faltered, and she felt him stagger. Unfortunately, the blanket impeded her long enough for him to recover and regain his grip. Next time when she swung, she only caught part of him. Even so, he shocked her by throwing her aside.

She tripped over the generator and fell so hard that the stars swimming in her head began to wink. She heard a screech of metal and the driving beat of the music. Then, as if her brain was lit by nothing more than a single candle, the wind swooped across her cheek and extinguished the flame.

SHE SANK THROUGH murky blackness and emerged in a red and glistening world. There was blood everywhere, and somehow she was standing in the middle of it. She had a scalpel in her hand and scrubs on her body. The bull was dead. She knew it but couldn't see the animal.

Hawley charged in, covered with blood and shouting. He tore aside crumpled metal to reach her. He wanted to kill her, and anyone who got in his way. Except the only people in his way were already dead, and by removing the broken seats and overhead racks, he was actually freeing her.

"You're gonna pay, lady. I'm gonna make you."

She heard a scuffle and a lot of swearing. Then the metal wall fell, and McBride held out his hands to her. Thank God.

He helped her navigate the rubble and the bodies. One woman had been impaled, another crushed. The third, a man, had died right in front of her. Another man had crawled out of the rubble, then bled to death on the rocky slope.

Shadows slunk in. McBride kept her ahead of him. She wanted to stop and rest, but he took her by the arms and shook her to keep her going.

Black mist combined with shadows to create an eerie fog.

"Alessandra, wake up! Come on, wake up!"

She knew it wasn't McBride who shook her like a rag doll, but the voice sounded familiar.

"Wake up!" it ordered again.

She surfaced slowly and with great reluctance because her head hurt more beyond the darkness than within it.

"We have to get out of here. The guy took off, but he could come back any minute, and I don't think I'd win if he jumped me right now."

Raven's rusty voice penetrated the cracks. It came with wind and music and the faintest tinge of fear.

Alessandra forced her eyes open. "What...?"

Raven hauled her out from behind the generator. "Man's all I know. He whacked me a couple times outside my truck. Whacked Rip when he came flying in to defend me. I think he dropped his gun in the well when he went to hit Rip. He took off when I ran in here with a piece of lead pipe. I didn't see his face, but he's gotta be nuts. We need to move. Could be he's gone for another gun."

Rain from the tips of Raven's hair dripped onto Alessandra's face. Only about half of what she said registered. But the urgency got through.

She struggled to sit, made it to her knees and swayed. She wanted to topple facedown and sleep for a year, but Raven tugged her to her feet.

"I yelled at him, told him I called a deputy," Raven said. "Maybe he believed me."

They stumbled to the door and out into the sheeting rain.

"Rip!" Raven released Alessandra and ran to the unmoving animal.

Alessandra took the other side, lifted the dog's eyelids, listened to his heart.

"He's breathing." More alert with chilly water sliding down her neck, she regarded the blurred landscape. "We need to get him into your truck."

"I'll do it."

Raven hefted the animal while Alessandra kept watch. Was that movement she saw on the far side of the trees?

She breathed in and out, closed her eyes to clear them and focused on a clump of towering pines.

"He's in," Raven announced. "I think he's coming around. He barked a little. What is it?" she demanded when Alessandra bent low to peer through the trunks.

"Is there a road back there?"

"Way far back, yeah. It's not much of one anymore, but people use it sometimes."

"I see a bus, a yellow school bus, with something red painted on the side."

"So?"

"McBride and I saw a bus like that a few days ago outside a motel."

Raven leaned forward. "Okay, I see the ass end. But again, so what? You think whoever attacked us is driving a school bus?"

"I'm not—" Alessandra hesitated. "I don't know. Maybe not."

Once again she felt the man's hands on her, heard his voice growling in her ear. He'd been furious.

Who, though? Who'd been furious?

Rory was gone. He claimed he didn't own a rifle. But someone other than Eddie had shot at them outside Ruth's motel. And now there was a bus like the one she and McBride had used for cover from the shooter back in Wyoming.

One thing was certain, she realized with a shudder. She'd been wrong before. The nightmare wasn't over.

Chapter Thirteen

McBride needed to be angry. Not at Alessandra, or Raven, or even at Rory Simms. He was angry at himself for not listening to his gut when it told him something more was happening here than he'd originally thought.

More than a single shooter. Although he'd tried to convince himself, he'd never quite believed that the second guy had been dispatched by Casey Simms. Hell, the second guy had killed the first.

Yes, that could have been an arranged hit, because Casey was nothing if not two-faced, but every instinct McBride possessed—not to mention the two threatening emails Alessandra had received from a mysterious person called YAMAN—had shouted at him to beware.

The door opened and Alessandra came into the room, drying her hands on a white towel. "Rip and Raven are good, the storm's widespread and getting worse and the sheriff will be back in a few days. Apparently his mother's doing much better."

"Great, I know and I talked to him this morning." Capturing her arm, he tipped her head back for a look, not an easy thing to do by battery lamp.

"I'm fine," she said before he could ask. "No double vision, no blurring, no glitches in my memory. Raven saw the tail end of the yellow bus through the trees, so no hallucinations, either. Unfortunately." When his gaze flicked to the window, she sighed. "We're not staying, are we?"

"Do you think we should?"

"Yes, because there's safety in numbers. No, because whoever that man was, he could have killed Raven and Rip as easily as he knocked them out."

"More easily." McBride ran a thumb over her cheek, then reluctantly let his hand fall. "Which, if you want to put a positive spin on this, suggests that it's us he wants dead and not everyone in his path."

"He killed Eddie, McBride."

"That could have been an accident. There was a lot going on that night. Rifle shot took out the motel window to get things started. He might not have realized Eddie was there at first. A gun went off nearby, he responded, hit the wrong person."

"Wrong from Eddie's perspective, not ours."

"Yeah, well." He gave her eyes another inspection and motioned toward the bathroom. "Are you packed?"

"Leaving tonight, huh? I was never unpacked." She started to turn, but swung back. "Please tell me we're not sleeping in the truck."

"Would you rather sleep in a puddle?"

"Okay." She held up her hands. "But just so you know, last night notwithstanding, I'm back to hating you. Where are we going?"

"Rapid City, as fast as Moe's truck will take us."

"Does that mean I can go home?"

"No. And before you ask, we won't be using the interstate, either."

She fired a grim dagger at him. "I really hate you, McBride. What's wrong with major highways? If he can't catch us, he can't hurt us."

"Even a bus can move on good roads, Alessandra."

"All right, rewinding to your positive spin, why not stay in Loden but keep away from everyone? And don't say that's not possible."

"I was going for optimism with that positive spin remark. Pretty much, when a killer wants you dead, he or she will do what's necessary to get the deed done. Raven and Rip got lucky."

He saw the battle taking place in her mind. Since he already knew which side would be the victor, he slung his backpack over one shoulder and picked hers up by the straps. "It's getting late, storm's peaking, the whole town's gone dark. We'll never have a better chance to slip away undetected."

"Can we at least buy a tent?"

"No need," he told her.

"McBride…"

"Think about it." He made a final visual sweep of the street below, or at least what he could see of it through the pouring rain. "Whoever this guy is, whatever he wants, our first priority is to get him out of Loden before he decides to go postal. But running from him for any length of time won't accomplish a thing. He'll just keep following us, as he's apparently been doing all along. I did some checking while you were examining Raven's dog and while I could still make a connection. According to my source, your pissed-off bull breeder's been drowning his mad in liquor on his ranch near Rapid City for several days now."

"Well, that's…"

"His son-in-law, Ryder, hasn't been seen since early Friday morning."

"Did your source ask Hawley about him?"

"Yeah, he says Ryder's gone fishing."

"Where?"

"Hawley claims he doesn't know. The cop—my source—who questioned him, thinks he does, but is refusing to talk. That could mean any number of things, one of them being his son-in-law's off on a private vendetta."

Alessandra walked ahead of him down the barely lit hotel corridor. "The guy who grabbed me was tall. At least that's the impression I got. I had to swing upward to hit him."

"So did Raven. She said she saw part of a plaid shirt before he knocked her out. She thought he was probably six to eight inches taller than her. You're five-seven, she's five-eight. That puts him upward of six feet."

"Ryder's upward of six feet."

"Yeah, you said."

"But you haven't yet." At the top of the stairs, she turned to plant a hand on his chest. "Where are we going?"

"The sheriff has a getaway in the Black Hills. The dispatcher—his mother-in-law—is worried about us. She gave me the keys."

"Halfway to home sweet home. I love you again." She gave his shirt a tug and his mouth a kiss that made him want to say screw safety and haul her back to their room.

But that wouldn't tell them who YAMAN was or why he wanted Alessandra dead, along with him and some other person whose name she hadn't heard. All they knew was that the guy probably drove a yellow school bus, was good with an assault rifle and was unlikely to be connected to Casey or Rory Simms.

Connected to Frank Hawley? Not much more likely

in McBride's opinion, despite his son-in-law's unknown whereabouts.

No matter how he ran it, he kept coming back to that yellow bus—and a very different bus before it.

He'd parked Moe's truck in an alley mere feet from the back of the hotel. A gust of wind drove rain and debris inside when he opened the door. A quick scan of the area revealed no other vehicles around. Only overturned trash cans and a dozen or so beer kegs.

"When I say go," he told Alessandra, "run. Stay between me and the truck, and use the driver's side door. Ready?"

"I wish you'd ask me a question I could answer."

"Go."

It only took a few seconds to slosh through the ankle-deep water, but those seconds felt like minutes. And the situation didn't improve once they were inside the truck.

Less than twenty feet in front of them, headlights flared. McBride swore, got the engine started and shoved Alessandra's head down. Slamming the truck in Reverse, he floored it backward down the alley.

The blast of rifle shot from the opposing vehicle came as no surprise. The return fire from the passenger's side of Moe's truck did.

"What the hell are you doing?" he shouted.

Alessandra fired again. "Just get us out of here, McBride."

Easier said than done since the alley was long and only had a few leads to the street. He found one at last, zipped across it, swung the wheel over and threw the truck into second gear.

Another blast hit the box, a third the side of the town's bank.

McBride ran the options in his head. Stop, bail and

try to shoot the guy's tires or let the bastard chase them out of town.

A string of late-night partiers weaving across the road settled the matter. A confrontation here was too dangerous. He'd draw YAMAN away from Loden and see what developed from there.

As for Alessandra...

He glanced over while she raised the window. "You know that was a spectacularly dangerous thing to do, right?"

"I learned from the best." Finger combing the hair from her face she tied it in a long ponytail, then picked up the gun and looked behind them. "Where did he go?"

"I'd like to think one of your bullets crippled him, but I'm not holding my breath."

"I might have hit a tire."

"Or he could have killed his headlights." He gestured at her shoulder bag. "Try Larry's number. After I called Rapid City, I couldn't make a connection by landline or cell."

"Cell tower's probably damaged, and the landlines went down right after lunch. But why call Larry and not one of the deputies here in— Never mind. Larry, it is."

"I need to talk to Ruthie."

"Motel Ruthie? Why... Ah, got it. Yellow school bus. The driver who rented night space in her lot. I wouldn't count on her remembering his face."

He sent her a level look and saw her lips curve.

"Okay, maybe she will. Larry did say the guy took off without paying." She regarded the screen. "No connection yet."

"Try again in a few minutes."

"I still think we need help, as in highway patrol officers or state troopers."

McBride grinned. "After all we've been through, you still have no faith in me."

"I have all kinds of faith in you. I just want to back it up with some extra firepower, seeing as we have no idea who this guy is or what his overall agenda might be. I wish I could…"

He cast her a quick look when she trailed off. "What?"

"Not sure. I have a feeling there was something familiar about the man. It's way out there on the edge of my brain. I see the outline like a ghost, but it disappears before I can turn it into anything solid."

"Is it something you saw or something about his voice?"

She thought for a moment, but shook her head. "It's too elusive. I couldn't see much, though, so it can't be visual. It must have been his voice. All I know is that he wants you, me and at least one other person dead. 'One death for another and another and another,' he said. Apparently we're two of the others he's focusing on."

"So who's the one?" McBride glanced in the mirror. No headlights so far, and they were approaching the junction that would take them east.

"Leopard," Alessandra gave the word a curious inflection. "I know that's not the word he used, but it sounded like it with the thunder. And he's driving a school bus, McBride. Why?"

"Setting the leopard part aside for the moment, what's the only thing you and I have in common that involves death?"

"The bus accident. I figure it must be relevant. But I still don't understand why. Neither of us killed anyone that night, or caused anybody to die."

"That we know of."

"Well, that makes me feel better." She stared into the

darkness, let her mind slide back. "When the bus rolled, the guy beside me went one way, and I went the other. The overhead compartment broke loose and pinned him in a corner. I'm pretty sure it severed his legs, but I couldn't see under all the debris. And I couldn't move it. He didn't last long, I remember that."

"Do you know anything about him?"

"Plenty. His name was Ivan Gregov, but he called himself John Gregory. He was born in Saint Petersburg, Russia, back when it was Leningrad. He was thirty-eight years old, and his favorite movie was *Rocky.* He was gay. He had a life partner who'd been working in Chicago for six months. I met his partner after the accident. He's American, likes to run marathons and sells insurance. His name's—"

McBride looked at her. "You remember all that, but you forget his partner's name?"

"I know his partner's name, McBride." She brought her eyes around to his. "It just didn't strike me until now that it almost fits. The guy who grabbed me said something that sounded like 'leopard.' The partner of the man next to me who died was Leonard. Allan Leonard."

IT DIDN'T PROVE anything, Alessandra reminded herself for the next thirty miles. She wasn't even sure that leopard or Leonard was what she'd heard. The thunder had been directly overhead at that point, and she'd been thinking more about how to escape than what her captor was saying.

Of course, none of those things stopped McBride from grilling her like a prosecuting attorney. But no matter how many times she went through it, she couldn't come up with a single reason why anyone would want to kill her, McBride and possibly the partner of a dead man from Russia.

"Maybe John Gregory née Ivan Gregov was a spy," she suggested, and picked up her BlackBerry again. The right tires bounced through a pothole and almost sent the device flying from her fingers. "Someday you'll have to explain to me what it is you have against maintained roads."

"Believe it or not, the route we're taking is more direct than a highway." He managed to avoid the next hole—which was fortunate in Alessandra's opinion since they'd probably have lost the truck in it. "We're also driving with the storm. Anyone following us will have a tougher time of it."

"So this is like a war of attrition."

"Or a demo derby."

"Last vehicle standing wins. Still no signal." Sitting back, she propped her feet on the dash, as much to keep herself from going through the windshield as to find a semicomfortable position in Moe's old truck. "It occurs to me, McBride, that you've never told me much about the night of the crash from your perspective. Details," she added before he could object. "You were in that place at that time because…"

"An undercover murder investigation I was on went south."

"No more to it than that, huh?"

"Plenty more, but that's all you need to hear."

"It's all I need to hear about the investigation."

She saw a muscle jump in his jaw. "I don't want to talk about my father."

"And I didn't want to come on this road trip with you. But I did. He was in Chicago, wasn't he? With—what would she have been, wife number three?"

"I never bothered to count."

"Your father showed up, you took off. Okay, a case went bad, and the whole cop thing was getting to you, I understand that. But you didn't leave the city because of those things." When he still didn't speak, she softened her tone. "I could have learned the truth, McBride. Your partner and his wife liked me. Your partner might not have said anything, but his wife would have if I'd pressed her. I didn't because I wanted you to talk to me, confide in me. But you never did, and while I probably should have, I didn't press you, either."

"Until now. In the middle of nowhere, in the middle of a storm with a murderer on our collective ass."

"In other words, 'My business, not yours, darlin'.'" She averted her eyes and tried the phone again.

They'd reached a smoother section of road. Setting an elbow on the window, McBride ran a finger over his lips and slid her a half-lidded look. "It doesn't help me to talk about him."

"How would you know?" she asked, barely glancing his way. "You never do."

"I prefer to disconnect totally. He is what he is, I am what I am. We're fine with that."

"Talking about him isn't the same as connecting with him."

"I'm pretty sure I said total disconnect, as in I see myself as not having a father."

"Being a vet and knowing that red stuff in your veins is blood and not ice water, I'll argue that point. But later, because—" She held the phone she'd been playing with perfectly still and put it on speaker. "It's ringing."

"Hello to you at last, Alessandra." Larry sounded enormously relieved. "I thought some catastrophe must have occurred way over there in Wyoming. Are you two all right?

"We're good." She glanced behind them. "For the moment. Uh, we need a favor." She explained about the bus.

He listened, but even through the hiss and crackle of poor reception, she felt his mounting tension.

"I knew it," he exclaimed. "I said to Morley when we found it there'd be a link."

"Get the short version," McBride said in an undertone. "Fast."

Alessandra raised her voice. "We're in the middle of a storm, Larry. You're on speaker so McBride can hear you, too. We need the details before the connection cuts out."

"We found a man's body," Larry replied. "Actually, Ruthie found it. She was sweeping and noticed a bad smell coming from the woods. She followed the wind to an old shed that used to be a smokehouse. Opened the door, and there he was."

"What man?" Alessandra really had to shout now to be heard. "Did she recognize him?"

"Recognized and felt downright bad for what she'd been thinking," he shouted back. "It was the man driving the old school bus. Fiftyish fellow, wore his hair in a long gray braid."

"How did he die?"

"The way you'd probably figure. Rifle shot to the chest."

Out of her element, Alessandra turned toward McBride. "Shouldn't you be doing this?" she whispered to him.

"You know what to ask." He swerved around a large, fallen branch.

"Did anyone see or hear anything, Larry?" she asked.

"Not a soul and not a thing so far. Norm, Ruthie's son, did come across a truck in a ditch near the motel. Beat-up old thing, but it has a decent engine. Doesn't make sense why someone would abandon it."

"Email pictures," McBride instructed Larry. "Truck, body, smokehouse."

Alessandra added, "Was there anything in the truck to identify its owner?"

"Clumps of dirt and grass. Some leaves. Lotta dead bugs, bits of food—dried-up fries and Fritos and such. No papers, though, and nothing in the glove box. County sheriff's running the plates. He reckons they could be stolen. No report that the truck itself was... Hello, Alessandra? You there?"

"I'm here. Send the pictures, okay? Larry?" She moved the phone around to pick up a signal but found none. "Looks like that's it for now. I still think we should have called for backup first." At another booming noise she flicked her gaze to the roof. "Please tell me that was thunder I just heard."

"If it isn't, he's got a cannon on that bus."

A chill crawled down Alessandra's spine and spread to her limbs. "You were right about leaving Loden. Raven and Rip really did get lucky. He's not going to give up until we're dead, is he?"

"No."

The word was like a punch to her midsection. It made breathing difficult and thinking nearly impossible. Which might explain why McBride had never wanted to talk about his work.

Pushing on a tight spot between her ribs, Alessandra

stared into the turbulent darkness in front of them. "I have to tell you, McBride, compared to most of us, your job really sucks."

SERENDIPITY. THAT'S HOW he saw it. When he could see anything beyond the two of them dead.

He'd waited so long for this, so damn long. He'd suffered and acted and suffered again. He'd plotted and planned and thought it through in great, bloody detail. Then, the very night he'd gone to do it, up had popped a wild card.

Yet with that card had come a bonus, so he'd let it play out, bided his time, became a shadow.

He'd followed the hit man who'd been following them—he didn't care why. He'd stolen a bus. How perfect was that? Total serendipity.

Lately, he'd been following them on his own. He'd almost had her. He *had* had her. He would again, too. And the cop after that. And then...

No, stop, back up. One person at a time. The vet came first, because she'd started the nightmare. If it wasn't for her...

The thought cracked apart. A blinding red haze filled his head, clouded his vision. The only thing it didn't cloud was the knowledge that drove him.

YAMAN.

Chapter Fourteen

"I'll never understand why anyone would do this to an animal." In the kerosene-lit interior of what had the potential to be a lovely mountain cabin, Alessandra stroked the muzzle of an elk mounted above the fireplace. "It's inhuman."

"That's what makes it legal, darlin'." McBride dropped their packs in a corner, checked the front window, then his Glock. "Mourn the dead later. Chances are good we'll have company before long."

Giving the elk a final stroke, she went in search of another lamp. "How could anyone have followed us in the dark through all that rain? We could hardly see the road—if that actually was a road we were on for the last fifty miles. We also have a four-wheel-drive truck. He's driving a bus."

"Think bug, Alessandra, the nonaudio kind. I don't know how close he is to us. I want a quick separation in case he's right on our heels. It'll give us a slight advantage if I can plant the truck and draw him to it."

"Shouldn't I be coming with you?"

"If he is right behind us, I don't want him shooting at you."

"Right, better he shoots at you, because no way could he hit you twice, right?"

A faint grin appeared. "Something like that."

He left her with that and a strong desire to throw something at his head. A cushion would do, but since the only available cushions appeared to be covered with horsehair, she refrained.

McBride returned a few minutes later, extinguished the lamp she'd just lit and handed her a pair of extra bullet clips. "Keep the blinds down and the curtains drawn. They're blackouts so there shouldn't be a problem. Keep your gun out and don't light a fire until I get back. Bug," he said again, and although she wished she could argue, she understood that if she went with him, he'd only worry about her more. Still....

"You realize you'll be stranding us in this cabin."

"Only temporarily."

"What if he sabotages the truck?"

"He'll still have to find us."

"*Sans* bug." She smiled. "We hope."

McBride shrugged. "I don't think he's been close enough to our personal effects to slip a tracking device inside, but just in case, while I'm gone…"

"You're a pillar of comfort and reassurance, Mc-Bride."

He walked over to her, his eyes dark, intent. "This wasn't supposed to happen, Alessandra. Not any of it. But if things hadn't gone down the way they did, it probably would have been a whole lot worse. For both of us."

"He'd never have gotten you, McBride."

"But he might have gotten you." He brushed the hair from her temple, slid his knuckles over her cheek, then wrapped his fingers around the back of her neck and brought her mouth up to his.

It wasn't a long kiss, but it smoldered and stirred and seeped right into her bones.

He was gone before her head cleared with a quiet, "Back in twenty," that had her gaze shifting to the phone under the lamp—4:43 a.m. It was going to be a long twenty minutes.

Like it or not, however, she might as well use it to think. Time to revisit the trip that had taken her from Indianapolis to a ravine outside Chicago.

After a thorough search of their packs, she paced in an edgy circle around the room as the memories assailed her.

The bus driver had set her teeth on edge from the start of the trip. She remembered him telling her he didn't normally work that route, but the regular guy was "unavailable." Ergo, substitute driver. Though interesting, she set that aside.

The bus had filled quickly with a variety of people, from young to very old. A rude woman with a great deal to say had insisted on sitting in the front row. She'd wanted her daughter to sit next to her.

For the sake of a peaceful journey, the other passengers had shuffled around to accommodate them. Not that Alessandra had minded since it had taken her out of range of the leering driver and provided her with an interesting road companion. One who'd died several hours later.

His partner, Allan Leonard, had been shattered, but she didn't think he'd sued the bus company or attempted to cause problems for anyone else on board.

The driver had behaved like a jerk at the first rest stop. She remembered wondering if he had a bottle stashed under his seat; however, a postaccident blood test had come back negative.

After she'd rebuffed him, he'd tried his luck with two of the other female passengers, the third being a fragile young woman from Arizona. Everything about her had been pale, blond and soft. Except for the very firm objection she'd made to his advances.

Alessandra paused for a moment. It always came back to the same person, she realized, a replacement driver who hadn't gotten anywhere with the women on board, until a welder named Georgia, whom he'd managed to overlook, had strolled up and started flirting with him while he drove. Yes, she'd also died, but her death had occurred a month or so after the crash.

Alessandra glanced at her phone, sighed. Time was literally crawling by. McBride had only been gone for ten minutes.

She stopped pacing to listen, but thankfully all she heard was rain drumming on the roof.

She let her thoughts return to Georgia's story. What else did she know? She'd read about the woman. Why couldn't she remember the details?

Well, duh, she thought, and gave her head a mental shake. In a word, that would be McBride.

Life had taken her on a roller-coaster ride after she'd met him. The gorgeous, sexy, angst-ridden, bad-boy cop had surprised her with his first call. Did she want to go out with him? The man was everything she'd been looking to find—taste and experience, in one amazing package. How could she be expected to care what was going on in the rest of the city? The state? The world?

Pivoting, she tuned back into her surroundings. Still quiet other than the rain. And fifteen minutes since he'd left.

Meanwhile, back on the bus…

The rude woman who'd caused the fuss at the outset

had been crushed in her seat. Her daughter had survived, but died of a head trauma less than a day later.

Like John Gregory, the pale woman from Arizona—Anna or Abby?—had passed away on-scene. As she'd crawled out of the bus, Alessandra had glimpsed the shocked expression on the dead woman's face. Did that mean the woman had lived long enough to realize she'd been fatally impaled by a shard of glass?

Alessandra shoved the nightmarish question aside and continued to prowl.

An elderly man had succeeded in dragging himself through one of the windows before he'd expired from a number of internal injuries. A younger man from Tennessee had lost the lower portion of his left leg. The driver had walked away without a scratch.

There'd been a lengthy investigation afterward. Yes, the driver had been distracted, but on the mechanical side, some integral part of the undercarriage had developed a serious crack. As the bus veered into a sharp turn, the cracked portion of the suspension had snapped. No one could have saved it at that point. The vehicle had skidded sideways, slammed into the guardrail and gone for a slow, terrifying roll.

She stopped pacing, breathed out her frustration. All this reliving, and nothing new was coming to her. But there had to be something. And it had to involve McBride.

Settling on the arm of the sofa, she picked up her phone. McBride had been gone for twenty-three minutes…and her email alert was on. Maybe the storm was moving out of range.

Larry was the sender. He apologized for not attaching any pictures. Morley was having trouble with both his camera and his cell, so it might take a little longer than planned to get the photos uploaded.

He described the ditched truck as a rust bucket on four wobbly wheels, claimed it smelled like a sewer and, yes, the plates had been stolen—from a pickup in the parking lot of a bar on the outskirts of Rapid City. Alessandra did a startled double take when she read the location—half a mile from her clinic.

Drawing back, she struggled with the revelation. Half a mile? Her heart beat hard and fast in her throat. He'd been that close to her, and she'd had no idea, no clue. Unless McBride was wrong, and Hawley really was behind this, because he had, after all, threatened her verbally.

He'd also denied making any other kind of threat....

Okay, enough. She slashed a hand through the air, stared at the door. "Come on, McBride."

Nothing happened, except the rain sounded heavier now. In an effort to stem the fear fluttering around the edges of her mind, she focused on her email.

Joan, whose faith in McBride was unshakable, had sent a chatty message earlier that day.

She said Dr. Lang wanted Alessandra to return ASAP. One of their favorite black lab patients had given birth to four puppies. Unfortunately, another dog had swallowed a rubber ball. A check written for after-hours services had bounced, the bathroom plumbing needed work and Joan's bunions were killing her. All in all, a typical day at the clinic, one that brought Alessandra a moment of much needed relief.

Then the lock on the door rattled. As her moment vanished, fluttering fear whipped up to full panic.

Sliding from the sofa, she braced her forearms on

an ottoman, gripped her gun in both hands and ordered herself to remain calm.

If it was McBride, he'd call out to her. But would she hear him above the rain, the wind and the roar of blood in her ears?

They should have arranged a signal, a double-triple knock or something equally simple.

When the lock rattled again, her heart raced out of control. McBride had a key. If it was him, he'd use it.

She swore, softly, succinctly. Her wrists threatened to tremble. No, not allowed.

Overhead, something landed on the roof.

Her eyes went up. A hot ball of fear climbed into her throat. Then, ten feet in front of her, the door burst open.

"Don't shoot!" McBride came in low and with a hand extended. He was soaked and muddy, and the sleeve of his jacket was torn from elbow to wrist.

No blood, Alessandra noticed. Exhaling in a rush, she let her head drop onto her outstretched arms.

He closed the door, leaned against it in a crouch, breathing hard. "Sorry, darlin'. I ran into an unfriendly barbed-wire fence and dropped the key. I thought about tapping on the window, but I didn't think you'd hear it above the storm. Short of shouting at you and alerting anyone in the vicinity, all I could do was break the lock."

She brought her head up just far enough to see him. "So now we're lockless, truckless and I sincerely hope bugless, and it's going to be light soon." A sudden thought struck her. "Wait a minute, shouldn't we be watching Moe's truck?"

"*I* should be watching. And I plan to."

Of course he did. "I see," she said. "And what will I

be doing in the meantime? Sitting here with the sheriff's wall-mounted friends?"

His smile contained a trace of absent humor. "It's an option. Not the one I had in mind, though. This area's riddled with caves. Most of them are dead-end holes in the rock face, but if you're inside one, no one can attack you from behind."

"That's a novelty."

He tucked his gun in his waistband and stood. "You have to trust me, or a least trust that I know what I'm doing. The dispatcher gave me a locally drawn map of the area."

"Did she? How enlightening."

He smiled again. "I know the tone of that stare, darlin'." Easing the blind aside, he ran his gaze around the clearing. "You're annoyed because I didn't let you in on the plan sooner."

The laugh that bubbled up had to be hysteria. "You know, I would be if I thought for a minute you'd actually planned any of this. But too much time spent with you lately leads me to believe you're strategizing on the fly."

A low-battery beep from her BlackBerry eased the tension. "There's still a signal. The weather gods are giving us a second chance to call for help, McBride. Since there's a man out there who wants us dead, don't you think we should seize it?"

"I did as I was approaching the cabin. Best I could give the trooper I spoke to was this location and a description of the spot where I left the truck."

He wasn't always communicative, she reflected, but he was always thinking. And, she seriously hoped, a full step ahead of the person gunning for them.

McBride wanted the cover of darkness for their trek,

so loading up a single small pack, they set off for higher
ground.

"The sheriff's mother-in-law told me there are several geothermal pools in the area." He boosted Alessandra over a huge fallen tree in their path. "She and
her husband come here in the fall, get naked and dive
in. Afterward, they meditate on the surrounding rocks."

"There's a picture."

"I'm trying to free up your mind with casual conversation. You can't think clearly if your brain's a mass of
knots."

"You want me to go through the bus trip again, don't
you?"

"Smallest detail could be key."

Although the rain had slowed to a drizzle, the path
was ankle-deep in mud. She stuck to the outer edge and
watched for tricky drop-offs.

"It was pretty boring, all in all."

"You said the driver came on to you."

"Me, the woman from Arizona and two or three
others. Georgia, the welder, finally decided to come on
to him. They were talking when the accident occurred."

"Georgia died a month later, right? But you don't
remember how?"

"I'm not sure. It might have been from a brain aneurysm. A condition similar to that, anyway. Not something that could have been arranged."

"So strike Georgia from any and all lists. What about
the driver?"

"He got lucky accident-wise, but I remember hearing he was the victim of a home invasion a few months
later."

"Anything come of that?"

"No idea." She looked up, way up at a steep wall of

rock. "We have to do this, huh? Climb in the dark and the wet, with no safety gear?"

"I'll be right behind you."

He was also carrying the pack, which left her arms free. Still, thirty-five vertical feet of craggy juts and ledges later, Alessandra was more than happy to hoist herself onto solid ground.

"Your father would be proud of you," McBride remarked, joining her.

She scrubbed her grimy palms along the legs of her jeans. "My father'd be appalled. I fired bullets at someone last night. You don't do that in his world."

"No wonder he hated mine so much." He motioned for her to start walking again and followed her. "What happened to the bus driver, Alessandra?"

"I think he eventually got fired for lascivious behavior." She tossed a look over her shoulder. "Told you he was a lech." Then she halted so abruptly, McBride almost knocked her down. "Lech," she repeated as she spun to face him. "Lecher. That's what it was. Lecher not leopard. 'One death for another. And another and another and another.' There were four 'anothers,' McBride. Then he said, 'Yours, your cop husband's, that bastard lecher and…'"

"There was an 'and,' as well?"

"Yes. Four 'anothers,' a 'lecher' and an 'and.'"

"And the bus driver, the alleged lecher, was the victim of a home invasion."

"Yes, but that invasion was years ago, McBride. After the crash, and before he was fired, but still far enough back that it's probably not connected to what's happening now."

"Don't count on it."

"You do know we're talking five, maybe six years here."

"Home invasion's one thing. Armed home invasion is another. Think theft, armed robbery and possibly attempted murder in terms of prison sentences."

"The last two would carry much stiffer sentences." She walked backward on a level patch of ground. "Are you saying the guy after us could have been the home invader and could have subsequently gone to prison for attempting to murder the driver of the bus?"

"It would explain the time lag. Someone invades the driver's home with a weapon, gets caught, goes off to prison. Driver recovers emotionally, life and time go on. Home invader's released. Nothing's changed in his head. He moves forward with his plan."

"About which we're still in the dark."

"Good point." He glanced at the sky, then turned her around and gave her a nudge. "Speaking of, it's getting light. We need to keep moving."

At the pace he set, and given the difficult terrain they were covering, moving was all Alessandra could do. But while she might not be able to think in clear and concise lines, she could let her mind sift through snippets of other memories.

A picture of the rude woman continued to pop up in her mind. She couldn't be involved herself since she and her daughter were dead, but there she was in Alessandra's head—loud, demanding and disruptive.

After several minutes of trudging, they reached the spot where McBride wanted to be—within sight of Moe's truck, yet not close enough to be seen.

They crouched on the rim of an embankment so he could listen, observe and undoubtedly run down a long list of what-ifs.

Alessandra asked, "Don't you think I should—"

McBride cut her off with a raised hand. "Answer's no."

"But two guns are better than one."

"I doubt if Eddie would agree with you."

"So you expect me to cower in a cave while you take on a man with a scoped rifle. Honest to God, McBride, I can see the testosterone whizzing around your head."

"If that's all you see today, be happy. Now do me a favor and don't argue."

She made a sound—part frustration, part exasperation and, to her annoyance, part fear. She didn't like caves. They reminded her of root cellars, specifically the root cellar under Grandmother Norris's farmhouse, into which she'd accidentally locked herself as a child. Six hours of imaginary demons later, her parents had found her huddled in a corner, surrounded by every jar of homemade fruit, jelly and pickles she'd been able to reach. Her monster shield, she'd told them.

There'd be no preserves in a cave. Then again, there'd been no McBride in her grandmother's root cellar. Given a choice and in spite of everything, she'd go with McBride every time.

"You're worried, aren't you?" she said as she stood. "Are you afraid he knows what we're doing?"

"He might. He strikes me as a man who's insane, and insanity seldom takes a logical path. It's hard to outthink someone like that." He nodded up and to her left. "Mouth of the cave's over there."

Alessandra hiked ahead of him on the overgrown path. As always, he had her back. Bushes and brambles crowded in on both sides. The drizzle had turned back into rain, and as it had done last night, the wind kicked up to gust and swirl around them.

A leafy branch slapped Alessandra's face. She pushed it aside and glanced downward. Staggered clumps of trees and bushes stretched along the embankment to the road below. Spying a movement, she bent for a clearer view.

"McBride, stop. Look." Snagging his arm, she tugged him to her level. "There, where the spruce trees form a tight circle. You can see the back of it." Her fingers dug in as terror streaked through her. "It's the yellow school bus."

Chapter Fifteen

"Don't move," McBride said. "Not a muscle."

Alessandra wasn't sure she could have if she'd wanted to.

Thankfully, they weren't wearing bright clothes. They could blend in with the trees and— What? Wait until the shooter noticed them? They were only minutes away from daylight, he had a sighted rifle and there was no sign of a state trooper.

She'd stopped breathing. She realized it when her vision began to drift in and out. Exhaling carefully, she followed McBride's stare.

Strong gusts of wind bowed the small trees in front of them. For an instant, they had an unobstructed view of the vehicle's back end. Without warning, McBride shoved her to the ground and whipped out his gun.

Three shots from close by struck the pine behind her. Alessandra heard the thwacks and actually saw the areas where the bullets stripped the bark.

"Cave," McBride ordered. Blocking her from sight now as they ran, he engaged the shooter until they reached the opening.

"Go, go!" He endeavored to pull her around him as she scrabbled through his pack for a flashlight.

Yanking it free, she shone the beam in a broad half

circle ahead of them. "There's nowhere to go. This thing dead ends."

"Look down."

She did and saw nothing. Until...

Ten yards ahead and around a slight curve, she spied a boulder. Barely visible beyond that was a jagged patch of black.

A sinkhole, her mind said. While her senses resisted the thought, she knew it was their only hope.

"Wait." In a quick move, McBride doused the light and drew her down beside him. "Not a sound."

Again, she didn't breathe, but this time the omission was deliberate. She heard the scrape and thunk of someone jumping from the entry boulder into the mouth of the cave.

"I know you're here," a man shouted. His voice echoed off the damp walls. "This isn't my first choice, I want you to know that. But it'll do, it'll surely do. Only thing that matters is that in the end you're both dead. A death for a death, until I say it's done."

McBride tracked him. But before he could move, a shot rang out. Less than a second later, an explosion rumbled through the cave.

The rock walls at the opening blew apart with enough force to make the walls and floor shudder. The roar of cascading rubble was deafening. It created a shower of dust that billowed right to the back wall.

Even as Alessandra watched in stunned silence, the light, the trees, the wind and the rain vanished. Everything around them went black.

THEY MADE IT, heads down and coughing, to the sinkhole. McBride jumped in first, shone the flashlight down, then snapped it off and lifted Alessandra in with him.

The ground sloped, gently in some places, up to sixty degrees in others. They slipped and slid through musty darkness. At one point she thought they must be getting close to hell. Unless they'd bypassed it and were about to emerge in China.

Only a portion of the rocks and dust followed them down, and they had two flashlights, so at least they weren't descending blind. But several of the crawlways were tight, and once Alessandra actually got stuck. She didn't panic, because the alternative to going forward was going backward, and the entrance to the cave had been obliterated. Just as long as the slopes and crawlways kept appearing, she told herself they'd make it out.

Wriggling free, she hopped down and approached the top of another hole. Her heart sank when she heard the sound of rushing water.

She went to her knees, angled her beam downward. "Damn." Closing her eyes, she rocked back on her heels while McBride crouched to take a look. "I'm going to need a moment before I dive into that."

"What you need, darlin', is scuba gear."

So much for positive reinforcement. She stared up at the rock ceiling. "Was that dynamite he used?"

"That'd be my guess. He came prepared."

Why did she want to laugh? Whatever the reason, it couldn't be good.

Lowering herself to a cross-legged position, she pressed her forehead to the back of McBride's arm. "Pretty sure I'm having a Freudian moment. Or maybe it's a Jungian one. Either way I'm convinced that none of this is real. And not real equals nightmare—a projection of my deepest, darkest fears. Therefore, at some point I'm going to wake up in my bed in Rapid City and swear never to drink red wine on a Friday night again. Moment ended. Now pinch me."

McBride squeezed the back of her neck. "I have a better idea. On the off chance that this isn't a nightmare, let's work at getting out of here. Then if the pinching part fails, at least we'll be living your night terror as people who are free to move and react. The water will subside, Alessandra, once the rain stops."

"I know, I just needed that moment of absurdity to release some of the tension." She looked at him in the darkness. "I recognized his voice, McBride. I can't put a face to it, but I know it from somewhere."

"Is it Hawley or his son-in-law?"

"I don't think so."

"Someone from the bus?"

"Or after it."

"Like your dead seatmate's partner?"

"Or the rude woman's husband. It surprised me that she had one, but she did. Visualize Walter Mitty and you're there."

"Did I hear about this rude woman?"

She raised her head. "You don't tell me stuff, I don't tell you stuff. I thought about the trip a lot while you were relocating the truck. The woman and her daughter died. The only time I saw her husband was at the inquest. He didn't show much of anything emotionally."

"Did you talk to him?"

"I told him I was sorry for his loss."

"Was he?"

"Sorry? For the loss of his daughter, yes. For his wife…?" She made an uncertain sound.

Since there was nothing they could do but wait, McBride drew her to the nearest wall and tucked her in beside him. Sliding an arm around her, he pillowed her head on his shoulder and set his chin on her hair. "Might as well be comfortable."

Her lips curved. "You're way better than a bunch of mason jars, McBride."

"Can't say I've heard that comparison before. In what way was the woman rude?"

"She made about fifteen of us play musical chairs. She and her daughter purchased their tickets separately and therefore weren't seated together. She was determined to sit at the front, and she wanted her daughter with her. I was across from them at first, but someone else wanted my seat, so I moved again. That's when I met John Gregory." Her eyes rose to the overhead rocks. "Do you think he'll assume we're dead, or as good as dead, and leave?"

"Eventually. He might give it an hour or two, but my guess is, he's thinking we won't get out."

"I'm not sure I'm thinking differently."

McBride's eyes gleamed when he looked down. "If I said that, you'd deck me."

"I'm out of my element here," she reminded him. "Also very, very tired. And scared. And worried. And hungry," she realized, giving his stomach a light punch. "Because you refused to stop at that all-night Cherry Bomb diner we passed sometime around midnight."

"Be glad we squeezed in a couple of hours of sleep."

"I am, but I still don't understand what you had against Cherry Bomb. Even my father used to cave and take me to the drive-through once or twice a year."

He glanced away, considered for a moment, then rested his head on the wall. "My father's second wife worked in a Cherry Bomb near Tulsa before they were married. He went into it with the express purpose of relieving the cashier of her money. He stuck a gun inside his jacket, walked through the door and knocked a loaded tray out of Mary Ellen's—future number two's—hands. The cashier got mad at Mary Ellen and told my father to take a hike. Their boss heard the yelling and stomped out of the kitchen." McBride's mouth crooked into a humorless smile. "That's when things got ugly."

ALESSANDRA DIDN'T SAY a word. She didn't miss one, either. Over the next two-plus hours she heard more about McBride's father than she'd heard in all the years they'd been together. The truth wasn't pretty, and he didn't like telling it, but finally, she had some basic knowledge of McBride's and his father's nonrelationship.

"No matter how you work it, darlin', my old man makes yours look like Grandpa Walton."

She tried not to smile. "That's a stretch, but I get the idea."

He shone his beam downward again. "Water's receding. The rain must have stopped soon after our homicidal bus thief blew up the front entrance. Another hour should do it."

She shifted position, traced a circle on his stomach. "Right about now I'd love a pepperoni pizza. From Toscana's, in Wriggleyville. Onions, extra cheese, mushrooms. Deep dish, not thin crust."

He picked up the thread. "A bottle of Chianti."

"Cherry cheesecake for dessert."

"Hot sex after dessert."

"That's not fair." She laughed. "I want food, and you're pushing my lust button."

"We still have an hour to go. Pizza and wine are out, but the hot sex has possibilities."

"You truly are a sick man, McBride."

"You think? Look in the backpack."

"You're joking. If you brought along a box of condoms…" She stopped as she looked in the pack. "You didn't bring condoms. You brought chocolate. Two big bars of seventy percent cocoa chocolate." Framing his face with her hands, she gave him a resounding kiss that echoed through the chamber and came very close to diverting her. But the ground was hard and damp and, well… Chocolate.

"You're too easy," he said when she tore off the wrapper and broke the first bar into pieces.

"Comes from my mother's side of the family."

Slipping one of the squares between her teeth, she climbed onto his lap and leaned in to offer him a bite. When he took it, she smiled, then set her hands on his hips and did a slow gyration.

"My turn to reveal. You met her, but did I ever tell you about my Aunt Angelica? She used to be an exotic dancer at a club in the Bahamas. It was called Gilt, and I have to tell you…" She let her mouth slide in temptingly close to his. "The club wasn't misnamed."

SHE MIGHT NOT HAVE seen it all, but Alessandra figured after more than three hours in a cave with McBride, she'd done most of it. Or as much as she'd ever need to.

They'd had sex inside a cave. A big, cold, wet cave from which they weren't yet certain they would ever escape. Like a last cigarette before the firing squad, they'd enjoyed each other's bodies. Except her mind still refused to believe they were going to die in there.

She'd managed to lose all sense of time. As predicted, however, the water level eventually dropped. When it did, McBride jumped into the hole up to his knees.

"If it can get out, there's a good chance we can, too.

Unless this underground river empties into an underground lake."

She said nothing, just sent him a look that made his lips twitch.

They began the arduous trek through the waterbed. As it had all along, the ground sloped downward. The passage narrowed and broadened several times, but thankfully never seemed to end.

Then they turned a corner.

For a suspended and vaguely surreal moment Alessandra watched the river tumble into an impossible abyss.

"I'm not seeing this." But she couldn't drag her gaze away. "A waterfall. In a cave." She shone her light down. Way down. "There's no bottom, McBride, just another bend that's taking the water deeper."

"Doesn't matter." He angled his own beam in the opposite direction. "There's light coming through some of the rocks up there."

Spinning, Alessandra pumped an imaginary fist. Yes! Now those rocks were small enough to move.

It required time and a great deal of effort, but one by one, the prison wall crumbled and a hole appeared. A little more pushing and shoving and soon it was large enough for them to squeeze through.

"Well, there was an adventure you don't have every day." She brushed off while he looked around. "Any idea where we are?"

"Not really, but we want to go east, which means we'll have to climb."

"I'm going to be so thin when this is over, I'll be able to pig out on chocolate from now until Christmas and not have a thing to worry about." She started off, still brushing bits of rock from her clothes. "Don't give me that get-real look, McBride. I'm a woman. I think about it."

"Uh-huh." He tapped her jacket pocket. "Think about that instead. You're beeping."

Surprised, she located her phone. "It's a text from Larry. He says the sheriff's people lifted three clean prints from that abandoned truck. They're waiting to hear if any of them can be identified. The truck itself was stolen from a Rapid City tow yard, so no help there." She scrolled to the end. "He's still working on sending the pictures you wanted."

An unexpected obstruction appeared at her feet while her eyes were still on the screen. "I don't want to look," she said aloud. But of course she had to. "That's not a wall, McBride, it's a minimountain. Did I mention that climbing isn't my strong suit?"

He wrapped his hands around her waist to get her started. "It will be when this is over. Climb, stick and keep telling yourself we'll get him."

She took a moment to prepare mentally, then huffed out a breath and began pulling herself up the craggy face.

"When you get to that ledge, stop and rest," he said from below. "I want to check the top first."

"We'll get him," she muttered. "We'll get him. We will get him... If we ever get off this wall that's the size of Mount Everest."

Not all the rocks were rough and the smooth areas felt slick beneath her fingers. She made the mistake of looking down once and had to stop for a minute to combat the dizziness that swept through her.

Get to the ledge, she told herself. Another ten feet, and she'd be safe. Ten, seven, five...

She reached up. As she did, the toehold supporting

most of her weight crumbled. She knew her other foot wouldn't hold her, but she had nothing solid to grab.

And nowhere to go, her startled mind realized, except down.

"DON'T MOVE, don't squirm, don't even blink," McBride ordered.

In mild shock Alessandra held herself perfectly still. McBride had caught her with his own body. Caught and somehow trapped her between himself and the rock wall. She had no idea why they weren't both lying at the bottom, but since they weren't, the least she could do was freeze and pray.

"Find a handhold," he said with amazing calm.

She groped and was finally able to wedge her fingers into a crack. Two cracks. Her foot located a protrusion, and for the first time in God knew how long, she released a shaky breath.

"Okay, that was really horrible." The trembling in her knees abated. "Did we lose much ground—or, well, altitude?"

"A few feet." He kissed the back of her head. "I'm going to let go now, darlin'. You ready to move?"

Did she have a choice?

She fixed her eyes on the ledge. It was still in sight and, thankfully, the tremors in the rest of her muscles were diminishing.

Take a deep breath, she told herself, and climb.

It took five minutes to reach the ledge. Those minutes felt like hours. And it had to be days since they'd left the cabin.

McBride scaled the remaining eight feet like the mountain goat he apparently was. Seeing nothing, he went to his belly and reached for her.

"Moe's truck should be just over the next ridge."

She caught his hands. "I don't like that word, Mc-Bride."

"What, 'truck'?"

"'Over.' Although 'truck' isn't a whole lot better."

He chuckled. "It's an easy hike."

On her knees and momentarily safe, she examined her scraped palms. "An easy hike to a truck with a tracking device attached to it, and someone in a stolen school bus possibly still keeping watch. Unless it really has been days since we left the sheriff's cabin, I'm still sensing a strong element of danger."

"It's been four and a half hours," McBride revealed. "Have faith, Alessandra. We'll be in Ben's Creek before dinner."

She didn't ask, just stood and started walking. The rain had stopped, and she wasn't dead. There'd be food in Ben's Creek, and a bed. If they were very, very lucky, there might even be some answers to questions like…

"What could you, me and a lecher possibly have in common?" she wondered aloud. "Beyond the bus accident?"

"I like to think not much, but obviously someone disagrees. Are you sure there was no other lecher on the trip?"

She turned, kept walking. "Now how would I know that?"

"Just making conversation, darlin'. Turn back around and get behind me." He pulled his gun out of his waistband. "We're closing in on the spot where the bad guy's bus was parked."

She waited below while he scouted the ridge. The sun had returned. With it came heat and teeming insect life.

Shedding her jacket, Alessandra tied it around her

waist and thought longingly of a rose-and-chamomile-scented bath, a really good pinot noir and—and what else? Not Cary Grant at this point. Not McBride, either, if she was smart. After this sample of his current job, she'd rather be married to a cop than a U.S. marshal—albeit, maybe not to a detective in Homicide, which McBride had been when they'd met.

Whoa, stop, back up. What was she doing thinking about this, anyway? She loved him, she always would. That didn't mean she could live with him again.

Even if part of her wanted to, she had more important things to think about. Like who wanted them dead, and why?

McBride returned to find her leaning against a pine tree, fanning herself with a large leaf.

"The bus is gone. Truck looks fine from a distance. No slashed tires or smashed windows."

"Any state troopers?"

"Not so far."

"I know you didn't have time to look for it earlier, but will you be able to find the tracking device before we leave?"

His grin had a dangerous edge. "Consider it done."

"What does that mean?" She stopped fanning, slid her gaze to his face. When he didn't reply, her eyes narrowed. "Don't do this to me, McBride."

"We need to finish it, Alessandra. He'll figure out we're not dead sooner or later."

"I know that, and I'm not going to be cliché about this. I'm not," she said when a spark of humor appeared. "I want it finished so I can go home, get another dog, go gambling with Joan and her sister and—oh, God, I don't know. Live my life, maybe?"

He took her hand, kissed it. "If you're done, there's more chocolate in the truck."

The laugh that rose felt good. "Any more sugar, and I won't need a truck to get to Ben's Creek."

"There's also a small grocery store a few miles south of here, or so the dispatcher's map says."

"You don't mind stopping?"

"Ten minutes. You buy food, I'll contact the state troopers."

That sounded reasonable, and yet... "You're very cheerful all of a sudden. Why?"

"Let's just say, some of my training hasn't been entirely by the book. Yeah, the guy can track us with the device he planted. What he probably doesn't know is that with a little tweaking and a lot of luck, we might be able to track him back." The glint in his eyes deepened to a frightening level. "One way or another, I'm gonna get that bastard, Alessandra. And when I do, he'll wish to hell he'd taken that stick of dynamite he used to blow up the cave entrance and blown himself up with it instead."

Chapter Sixteen

"You're back." Larry greeted them with open arms outside Moe's repair shop. "I was starting to think I'd never see you again."

"I can't tell you how many times we came close to making that thought a reality," Alessandra said as he smothered her in a crushing bear hug. She waved at Moe and Curly, who waved back, and at Morley, who wagged his remaining three fingers at her.

"Where's the truck?" McBride asked after he, too, had been firmly embraced.

"Yours is up and running, good as new. The one from the ditch got hauled to the county impound. Mayor's idea, not the sheriff's or mine. It's not a far drive. We can go there first thing tomorrow morning. Tonight's Moe's ninetieth birthday bash. We're using my barn, and you're coming, both of you." Larry stuck out a finger at McBride's dark expression. "No lip, no back talk, no saying it's too dangerous. I'll tell everyone to arm up and be on the lookout for strangers. Now, d'you want to stay at my place or Ruthie's motel?"

While both options appealed to Alessandra, thirty minutes later she found herself listening to the rumble of a generator and waiting for the water to heat inside Cheech's trailer.

The creek bed being marginally cooler than the stuffy interior, Alessandra waved McBride's hat and offered him an unperturbed smile as she walked back and forth in front of the metal steps.

"Don't give me that look, I know why we're here rather than at the motel. Have I complained? And no matter how pissed off you are, it's not my fault your double-duty transmitter's not working properly. Where do you think he is?"

McBride sat on the step of the trailer, knees apart, her recharged BlackBerry between them. "Last blip I got showed him halfway between the sheriff's cabin and here."

She tried to keep her stomach from coiling into slippery knots. "So he is en route."

"He could be heading back to Rapid City."

"But you don't think so."

"Not really." He trailed her with eyes she suspected she'd never be able to read. "Relax, darlin'. I won't let him hurt you."

"I know." She batted a blackfly with his hat. "I also know I'm overlooking some small detail about that bus trip. Something that ties you, me, the lech driver and another person together." Halting beside him, Alessandra angled her head so she could view the BlackBerry screen. "What's that picture?"

"The truck Ruth's son found in a ditch. Morley's not a great photographer."

"Give the guy a break. He wasn't working with the best subject. That thing's ancient. It's three parts rust to one part spit." Sitting on the step beside him, she peered over his shoulder. "It also looks vaguely familiar."

"Yeah?" He brought up a second shot. "Are we back to your bull breeder and his son-in-law?"

"God, no. Hawley wouldn't be caught dead in a junker like that." She made a waffling sound. "Ryder might, though. He fixes up old vehicles in his spare time, sells them and gives his wife the money. While she's off shopping in Minneapolis, he does his disgusting sex-on-the-side thing."

"Sounds like a gem of a husband. What does his father-in-law think?"

"Hawley doesn't care. Joan says he did the same thing to his wife when she was alive. She died of a stroke," Alessandra said before he could ask. "And don't forget—" she tapped his shoulders with her index fingers "—neither Hawley nor Ryder are connected to that bus accident."

"That we know of."

"Well, now you're just making things complicated."

"Name of the game in law enforcement."

"Does that mean we're going to Moe's birthday party tonight or not?"

He grinned. "Seeing as everyone's going to be armed up, anyway, and we've been using Moe's truck to run from a killer for the past few days, it'd be rude not to go."

"There's that word again. Rude. Even though she's dead, I still think that pushy woman's part of this. Am I being weird, McBride, getting stuck on an irrelevant point?"

"No point's irrelevant... What?" he said when she rested her forehead against his shoulder.

"We need to buy a present for Moe, and the party starts in a few hours. What might a ninety-year-old man want that he doesn't already have?"

"A beautiful twenty-eight-year-old wife with legs that go on forever and a butt that makes men's jaws drop.

Unfortunately, he can't have you, so he'll have to settle for a bottle of really good whiskey—which I'm told is the only thing he ever asks for and all the guests give him."

"I'm surprised he's made it to ninety. I guess we can stop at a store on the way to Larry's barn." She swatted a mosquito from her arm. "I hate to think how I look right now. All I know is that I feel like something a very big cat dragged out of a cave."

His answering smile held just enough danger that she scooted out of range.

"Keep your mind on the blips, McBride. Another round of sex with you, and I won't have the strength to party."

Her admittedly feeble protest might not have put him off, but an incoming call had him motioning at the trailer.

"Take your shower. It's the trooper I spoke to this morning. Maybe they've picked up our mystery bus driver."

And maybe Moe would live another ninety years, but Alessandra doubted it.

The water ran warm when she tested it, and felt delicious sliding over her limbs and down her back. She used the lavender-and-cream shower gel she'd bought in town, a shampoo with the same luscious scent and followed both with a silky body lotion that made her wonder why she hadn't lured McBride inside and— No, stop, she commanded herself. She had to stay firm. No more sex.

Why? asked an inner voice.

"Don't do this, Alessandra," she cautioned herself. "Find the madman first. Think about tomorrow—well, tomorrow."

The madman had almost certainly ditched his truck in favor of another man's school bus turned camper. Because it wasn't a rust bucket on four wobbly wheels? Or because it made some kind of symbolic statement?

She pictured the truck while she dried her hair. She'd seen it, or one very much like it, before. On Ryder's ranch?

Possibly, but Ryder hadn't been on the bus that crashed and, as far as she knew, he wasn't connected to anyone who had been.

Ah, but how much did she know about the passengers with whom she'd traveled? How much did she really know about Ryder?

Still, it didn't feel right, she reflected after a few minutes. Possible, but not probable.

She could see the truck in motion in her head. She could almost hear it sputtering. There was something else, as well, something Joan had mentioned in one of her messages....

"You ready?"

At McBride's question, the thought winked out and took Joan's message with it.

McBride did his usual five-minute shower and still wound up waiting for her to finish.

She'd bought ivory cotton pants and a really pretty halter top in town that afternoon. The top had a deep V front and not much of a back. She'd wanted to add in a pair of strappy red shoes with superskinny stiletto heels, but she had to get to and from Cheech's trailer on foot, so she went with the cream-colored ankle boots instead.

A spiffed-up Larry met them on the far side of the ridge. The sun had already dipped below the tree line. McBride kept his eye on the intermittent blips he was receiving. Alessandra endeavored to pin down at least one elusive memory. She thought about going through her emails again, but between the road conditions and Larry's driving, she didn't have a chance.

"I told Ruthie we'd pick her up on our way past the motel." Larry winked at Alessandra next to him. "She took quite a shine to you after you told her about that cure for Puddles's ringworm."

"It wasn't—" he hit a bump and almost caused her to bite off her tongue "—much. Uh, can we fit another person in here, Larry?"

"Can if you sit on McBride's lap. Pretty sure he won't mind."

McBride merely grinned and raised a brow at her.

"Now, I want you to tell me everything I don't already know," Larry went on. "I've got the gist, but I'm confused about the motive. Alessandra was involved in a bus accident seven years ago, and now someone wants the two of you dead."

"If you've got that straight, you know as much as we do." McBride checked his screen. "Transmitter's stopped working."

"For him as well as us, I hope." Alessandra braced for another series of potholes.

His phone beeped. Setting an arm on the seat behind her, he switched to email. "Interesting," he said as he read.

She answered Larry's questioning look with an unruffled shrug. "If you're waiting for an explanation, don't hold your breath. Garbo was positively chatty by comparison."

McBride's lips curved. "I heard that, darlin'."

"Which means the information he's receiving is intriguing, but not earth-shattering." She tipped her head toward the screen. "You know a man named Methuselah?"

Larry chuckled. "Some folks around here call Moe that."

"My Methuselah's eighty-four and still an active archivist for the Chicago Police Department." McBride scrolled to the end of the message. "I asked him to dig up any information he could on the man who was driving the bus the night of the crash."

"And he found...?" Alessandra asked.

"Nothing you haven't already told me. One thing he did discover is that the driver who was supposed to make the trip wasn't indisposed as he claimed at the inquiry. It came out later, and was subsequently hushed up by the bus line, that the driver you got had made a pass at his superior's wife during a company picnic. Your driver had been working a plum route. When word reached his superior about the pass, he was yanked off the good route and stuck on a less favorable one."

Alessandra nodded. "Okay, that is interesting, but I don't see—" Then a light went on in her brain and she did. "Someone who knew about the pass leaked the information to my driver's superior. Someone as in the driver who was supposed to make the trip but didn't."

"You should have been a cop, Alessandra." McBride switched the screen back to transmitter mode. "The driver you were meant to have was better at distances than the one you got—more in tune with the bus, more safety conscious, less inclined to be distracted and therefore more likely to be aware of potential mechanical problems."

"In other words, if the regular guy had been driving, there's a chance we wouldn't have crashed, no one would have died and maybe the crazy person who's after us now wouldn't be."

"It's a theory."

"Which could make the driver who didn't go the fourth person in the murder equation." Confusion swept in from all sides. "Does that mean Hawley and Ryder are axed as suspects?"

"Methuselah couldn't find a link between either of them and anyone on the passenger list. Doesn't mean there isn't one, only that if one exists, it's obscure. My opinion? They're not involved."

She massaged a temple that had begun to throb. "I wish that made me feel better, but all it does is tangle my mind up even more. Larry, look out!"

The old man had been turning his head to follow their conversation. At her warning, he jerked the wheel hard to the right, and wound up with a rear tire spinning freely over a very deep ditch.

"Norman, what the hell do you think you're doing?" he demanded when Ruthie's rail-thin son picked himself up from the other side of the road and loped over to them. "Jumping out of the bushes like that. I haven't forgotten about your ma."

The man, in his late forties with a long face and droopy eyes, clung to the truck. He tried several times, but couldn't seem to speak.

"He's hyperventilating." Alessandra pushed on McBride's leg. "Let me out."

"It's Ma," he finally wheezed. "Fell…in the lobby." He smacked the top of his head with his palm. "Blood, there's blood."

Larry scrambled out of the truck. "Ruthie's hurt?"

Norm looked like a bobblehead figure that couldn't

stop nodding. "I waxed the floors. Party shoes." He made a splatting motion.

"Show me," Alessandra began, and almost had her arm yanked out of the socket as Norm hauled her across the road.

A twisty path led to the rear of the old motel. He tugged her up a set of stairs, through the office and out to the front desk. He was so distraught that McBride had to pry his fingers from her wrist.

Alessandra knelt beside the woman. Ruth's complexion, she noted, was ashen.

Norm was frantic. "Is she dead?"

"No." Alessandra checked her pulse and eyes, then bent her head to listen to the woman's heart. "Beat's fast, but regular. She's definitely lost some blood. A doctor'd be good."

Larry waved his cell. "Doc Dyer's gone fishing for a week. I'm ringing his replacement now. Lucky for us, he's coming up from Lancer for Moe's party."

McBride made a wary circle of the room. "Can you stop the bleeding?"

"It's stopped on its own." She examined the woman for other injuries, then glanced at Norm. "This looks worse than it is. No bones appear to be broken. But I need some information."

Norm's head continued to bob while he answered her questions.

Ruthie was seventy-six, took pills for high blood pressure and smoked a secret half pack of cigarettes every day. Norm didn't think she'd ever had a heart attack, but suspected he might be having one, so when Alessandra was done with his mother could she please take a look at him. Apparently the replacement doctor from

Lancer had cold hands and the bedside manner of a drill sergeant.

Larry came over and gently eased Norm aside. "Doc's a good twenty minutes away." He gave Alessandra an encouraging pat. "Anything we can do for her in the meantime?"

"Is there a cot in the office?"

"There's a sofa. We could carry her in."

"We" translated to McBride, who had less trouble lifting Ruth from the floor than Larry did getting Norm to stop nodding his head. "Blood's scaring him, I think. I'll leave him here in Ruthie's chair and call the doc again."

McBride crouched next to Alessandra. "Do you need me?"

"No, but that question had an ominous sound to it. Don't you think she fell? The floors are slippery, and her shoes do have a three-inch heel."

"Is that high in the female world?"

"Depends on the female. For Ruth, I'd say yes." She took the woman's pulse again. "Please tell me you don't think she was attacked."

"There was blood on the corner of the lobby desk and a scratch in the floor next to it, so in my professional opinion, I'd say she fell on her own. Feel better?"

"Marginally." She laid Ruth's hand on her chest. "Her respiration's good, pulse is steady. She could have a mild concussion, but otherwise, I'd say she's doing well. Seeing as she's not a horse or a dog, however, I'd rather the doctor make the official diagnosis."

When Norm thumped his chest for attention, she sent McBride a vaguely humorous smile and went to have a look.

By the time the doctor arrived, daylight had faded

from the sky. Moe hobbled in behind him with Curly on his heels. Shortly after that, trucks and cars began pulling into the lot. People climbed out. Coolers appeared and were carried inside along with canvas chairs.

Larry returned to say that there were at least fifty partygoers in the lobby, early arrivals who'd heard about Ruth and figured they'd drop by for a quick look-see.

One of those party people had an old boom box that belted out Garth Brooks at top volume.

Alessandra found McBride behind the lobby desk. A woman with orange hair and cowboy boots was attempting to capture his attention, but while he made polite noises, he was fixated on the BlackBerry screen.

"Tell me something good." Alessandra eased the halter top away from her heated skin. Too many people in a small space with no AC had sent the temperature into the nineties.

McBride's response was preoccupied. "I haven't seen any sign of a yellow school bus."

"I'd call that good."

"Most everyone here knows how to handle a firearm."

"I guess that could also be construed as good under the circumstances."

"Several of them are already half-hammered."

The woman with orange hair offered a bleary smile and a sloppy toast before draining her whiskey glass.

"Maybe not the best scenario," Alessandra decided. "Any more blips?"

"Not for a while." He motioned for Larry to join them. "Killer's heading this way, though, darlin'. Could be on the doorstep if the last reading I got was accurate."

On the doorstep? Alessandra forced herself not to react. "So, no party for us. Is the tracker he's following still attached to Moe's truck?"

"Yes, and I parked the truck behind an old farmer's stand. If I leave now, I might be able to intercept him before he reaches town."

"I knew it." She jabbed his arm. "You never intended to go to Moe's party. You were going to ditch me in a barn with a hundred armed guests and trust that even if he did manage to slip past you, no way would he get past all of them."

"Safety in numbers, Alessandra."

"Only where I'm concerned, apparently, because inasmuch as I'll be surrounded, you'll be alone with two measly guns. Meanwhile, a crazy man who, by the way, wants both of us dead, will be counterplotting in his own deranged and nonlinear way. Said lunatic will also be in possession of an assault rifle, dynamite and God knows what other weapons. But you go to the party, Alessandra. Mix, mingle and be safe. That madman's as good as caught."

The barest hint of amusement lurked in the eyes that met and held hers. "I take it you don't like my idea."

She didn't know whether to punch him and be done with it or give in and laugh at the whole ridiculous situation. There was a homicidal maniac heading for—possibly even in—Ben's Creek, and here she was with a bunch of strangers who were dressed in their Sunday best, drinking toasts to a ninety-year-old birthday boy and packing everything from pistols to sawed-off shotguns.

Ridiculous won. A little too easily, if she was truthful.

"Okay, fine." She raised her hands. "Call's yours. I'll assume Ruth's accident put your plan on hold or you'd be long gone." At his level look, she sighed. "Do what you need to, McBride. Just don't expect me to play party girl and endanger innocent lives. I'll wait at Cheech's trailer or—"

The rest of her sentence simply died as an explosion ripped through the air. The force was so violent it rattled the windows and shook the foundation of the old motel.

Several people, including Alessandra, lost their footing and pitched sideways. In her case, she fell into McBride, who managed to catch and keep her upright even as he slammed into the desk.

The screams and shouts torn from terrified throats faded to stunned silence as the echoes died off and left only the heavy thump of boom-box music in its wake.

Alessandra stared at McBride, then thought of Ruth in the office and spun for the door. McBride caught her before she could take more than a step. When he spoke, however, she couldn't hear him.

Pandemonium erupted, filling the air with a din that very nearly outstripped the explosion.

Larry ran out of the back room on unsteady legs. "What the hell was that?" he shouted. "A bomb?"

"Gas leak explosion?" someone else speculated.

McBride drew Alessandra out of the chaos. "That was dynamite. He's here." He shoved his backup in her hands. "Take this. Use it on anyone who's not dressed for a birthday party."

"Where did he set it off?"

"Sounded like the woods." Snagging Larry's sleeve, he pulled him into the corner. "What's behind the motel, structure-wise?"

"Smokehouse, old outhouse, big old garage full of junk." He flapped a hand at Morley through the mayhem. "What do you want us to do?"

"Stay with Alessandra. Whoever he is, he wants her dead."

She grabbed him before he could disappear. "He wants you dead, too, McBride."

"I know." A gleam of anticipation appeared in his eyes. "Thing is, only one of us can get what he wants. And it's not going to be him."

HE DIDN'T WANT to leave her. His plan, such as it was, had backfired, but they couldn't run forever, and no way was he handing Alessandra over to a killer.

Other people ran with him into the darkness behind the motel. Most of them headed for a nearby farm. Some followed him and the acrid odor of explosive. Feet pounded through the trees as they searched for debris.

Slowing, McBride let the crowd go past. He glanced at the motel, still in sight, and attempted to put himself in the murderer's head. Never an easy task when dealing with someone who was insane.

Blow up a structure. Draw attention to the devastation. Hide. Watch from a safe distance. People rush past. Once they're gone, circle back.

Like the shadow he'd become so many times in his life, McBride melted into the darkness and worked his way over to a cluster of bushes and boulders.

The human noise receded. Insects and animal sounds took over. The odd shout still intruded, but he blocked them, homed in on what was closer, what might try to return to the motel.

Sticking to the shadows, he did that himself and doubled back. He saw Morley standing at the rear entrance and another man at the side. Larry would cover the front. There were three ways in and three people on guard.

McBride went down on one knee. He had two of the

three entrances in sight when he spied the pinpoint flame and the lightning-quick movement that sent it flying in an arc toward the back wall of the motel.

Chapter Seventeen

Together, the doctor and Alessandra lifted Ruth onto a makeshift stretcher and into a minivan for transport to the hospital in Lancer. Larry and a slightly calmer Norm flanked her as she returned to Ruth's office.

She had no idea what McBride was doing, only that it had to be dangerous, and if he didn't wind up dead, he'd be shot at least once before the night was done. By her. She was that angry.

Larry tapped a man she didn't know on the shoulder, and sent him to the front door.

"All's well, so far, Alessandra."

"No comment." Her mind whirled in an endless spiral. Unable to shut it down, she prowled the small room, BlackBerry in hand, and ordered herself to think past the confusion. When that failed, she opened her email and reread every message she'd received since leaving Rapid City.

"Something," she said aloud. "I know there's something." But she simply couldn't find it.

Larry started the coffee machine and made small talk to Norm about a vehicle-related issue. Alessandra regarded the wall clock, bit her lip, then decided to call Joan at home.

Her assistant answered on the first ring.

"Alessandra? Oh, thank God. I kept hoping you'd phone so I could hear your voice." Her own dropped. "You're in trouble, aren't you? Big trouble."

"You could say." She scanned Joan's latest email as she spoke. "We're back in South Dakota, but—"

"I knew it. I love McBride, don't get me wrong, but the one time I tried to contact you at my cabin, he read the call display, texted me and said messages only. Anything verbal would be distracting and dangerous."

Alessandra's eyes suddenly froze on the screen. "Uh, Joan?" A tremulous ball began to form. "I'm looking at your last email. You said a check for some after-hours work we did bounced."

"Oh, hon, that was just me being mad as a hornet and blathering on."

"It might be relevant." She thought back to that night in the clinic and remembered the rain, the gusty wind, the vehicle. "I have this picture in my head of an old truck, a rusty old truck."

"With a man and a dog inside." The concern in Joan's tone turned to indignation. "You want to know about the check he wrote? Well, I'll tell you. It was a bum all right, and so was he. Amos Smith, he called himself. Only had counter checks, he said, because he moved around so much. Taught me a lesson, that's for sure. There's more, too. Worse. I took some food to the local animal shelter yesterday after work, and what do you think I saw in one of the cages? A beautiful German shepherd with a white streak on his back in the shape of an arrow. Now, you and I both know that's not a common mark."

Alessandra's blood, already chilled, ran cold. "You found the dog—what was his name, Phoenix?—in a shelter?"

"Yes, I did. Now you tell me, what kind of person

brings an animal in for a late-night examination, writes a bad check, dumps the poor thing, then takes off for who knows where? A crazy person, that's who. That dog is…"

She continued to vent. Alessandra heard the buzz of words in her head, but since none of them registered, she lowered the phone.

A rusty old truck, rolling away from the clinic. As if a dense fog had suddenly lifted, the image of that truck came clear. Truck, dog—and man.

Except… She couldn't see the man's features clearly. He was an outline more than an actual image. He'd been tall and thin, she recalled, verging on gaunt. He'd had a prominent Adam's apple and hands that tended to fidget.

And he'd taken the dog he'd insisted she examine after-hours to an animal shelter.

The fear spiking inside her morphed into terror.

Smith, he'd call himself Smith. He'd come to the clinic when it was closed. Had he planned to kill her that night?

She swung around, saw Larry and Norm chatting and remembered she was on the phone. Raising it, she caught Joan's outraged tirade. "Going south, my foot. Weird galoot. I tell you, Alessandra—"

"Joan, stop," she interrupted. Blood roared like thunder in her ears. "Did Smith say anything that sounded odd?"

A protracted "Well…" was the last thing she heard before a second explosion rent the air, rocking the building from foundation to rafters. The floor beneath her gave a mighty heave and sent her flying into Larry, who staggered into Norm, who collapsed on the sagging sofa.

Dust and debris rained down, clouding the room and temporarily blinding them.

Somehow, Alessandra wound up on her hands and knees. Dazed and disoriented, she watched the office swim around her. Had she hit her head?

She thought she heard Larry groan and, coughing, pushed herself upright.

A thousand thoughts buzzed in her head, but only one came clear. Smith had trapped her. And that being the case, what might he also have done with or to McBride?

The door. She needed to find the door. Find McBride.

"Alessandra?" Larry made a hazy attempt to locate her. "Are you hurt?"

She spied his hand through the swirl of dust and reached for it. "I'm fine. Are you and Norm all ri—?"

The arm that snaked around her neck snatched her away from Larry's outstretched fingers. A gun with a very big barrel jabbed her under the chin.

"You back off, old man," a man's voice, trembling with fury, snapped. "You, too," he warned Norm. "Either of you move, you're dead."

Larry's alarmed eyes came clear. "You can't—" But Alessandra shook him off when the man holding her tightened his grip.

"Don't you tell me what I can't do. I'll kill her here in front of you if I want to. That's not what I want, but one way or another, she's gonna die. Question is, do you wanna die with her?"

"No," she managed to gasp as Larry's fingers curled into angry fists. "I'll go with him. Don't move, okay? Please don't move."

An obliging Norm didn't twitch a muscle or even blink. Larry seethed, but slowly lowered his hand.

Smith's rough voice came into Alessandra's ear. "Now you and me are gonna leave. We see anyone, you say the same thing you did here." He gave her throat a nasty squeeze. "Unless you want more people to die because of you."

More people to die?

McBride's name shot through her head. Her insides turned to ice.

She backpedaled swiftly, had to if she wanted to hold back the panic. McBride was fine. Smith wasn't referring to him. He couldn't be.

"Move," he ordered when she dragged her feet. "You and me got a date with your destiny." He kicked the door open all the way, shouted into the lobby. "I see one person twitch, hear one sound I don't like, this little lady's gonna have a great big bullet hole where her head used to be. I know someone's here. Come out where I can see you."

There was a quiet shuffle before a man covered in plaster emerged from the far side of the reception desk. He looked dazed, as if he wasn't sure what had happened.

"In there with the others," Smith instructed.

The man faltered but complied.

Smith's mouth moved in close again. "Now it's just you and me and your cop husband, Dr. Norris."

McBride wasn't dead. The relief that streamed into Alessandra's limbs made her go limp. But he hefted her up with the arm still locked around her throat and shook her to keep her moving.

His voice, a rasp of pure loathing, growled, "You killed her, as surely as if you'd held this gun to her head and squeezed the trigger." He rammed the barrel up hard under her chin. "You murdered my wife, Alessandra Norris. She died, and you lived, and that was all kinds of wrong. Even when it seemed you might still pay the price and die, along came a cop to rescue you."

"Who—?"

"Shut up." When his arm jerked, she saw black. "You just keep moving your feet. You'll see how it's gonna be soon enough."

He gave the damaged lobby door a vicious kick and yelled, "If you're out here, McBride, you best not try and stop me."

He twirled Alessandra in an abrupt one-eighty as he spoke, then braced his spine against the trunk of a tree. He waited for several silent seconds before winding himself around the base. A wall of bushes rose up, black and dense. He shoved her through to the other side and forced her to walk for several minutes, with his arm still choking her and the gun still digging into the underside of her chin.

Bushes turned to woods and back to dense bush. Finally, he thrust her through a tangle of vines and leaves into a clearing that might have been an access road once upon a time.

And there it was, the yellow school bus she'd been glimpsing off and on since the night they'd first come to Ben's Creek.

Wrenching the door open, he tossed her inside and flung her to the floor.

"It's serendipity." The gun shook in his hand as he slammed the door lock in place. "Now you pick yourself up, and sit right there, in that very first seat on the aisle. That's where she was when she died, so that's where you'll be when you die."

"Who are you?" Alessandra managed to ask.

Teeth tightly clenched, he leaned in so close that his mouth almost touched hers.

"My name's Penner, George Penner. My wife was

going to visit her sister in Chicago, but you changed seats with her, and she died."

She swallowed a shocked breath when he whipped out a butcher knife with an eighteen-inch blade.

Shoving the tip under her left breast, he let his lips curve into an evil smile. "You're getting it, aren't you, lady? You're starting to understand. It took you long enough. I sent you messages at your clinic, then more specific ones on the road. I kept hoping you'd figure some part of it out. Now you're here, and we're gonna finish it the right and only way. As you killed, so shall you be killed." His eyes glinted in the wisp of light from Ruth's flickering highway sign. "YAMAN," he said, and gave the blade a twist. "You're A Murderer, Alessandra Norris!"

IT WASN'T THE FORCE of the blast that knocked McBride off his feet. It was a section of metal fence that shot off its footings and came at him like a giant garrote. He avoided one post, but the more jagged of the two struck the side of his head.

He pictured Alessandra's eyes for a split second, then nothing.

Until…

"McBride!"

A hand slapped him with force. It shattered the blackness in his mind and sucked him from the residue with a blistering punch of pain.

He intercepted the next slap before it made contact. Everything spun except the thought that had been fueling him even as he'd gone under. Alessandra…

Larry's features swam in. "You awake?"

"Enough. Where is she?"

"I don't know." The old man's face crumpled. "Some

guy took her after the second explosion. I tried to follow, but Norm kept fighting me, said not to move or he'd kill us all. By the time I got loose, they were gone. And Cory in the lobby was only half-conscious. He didn't see anything, either. What're we gonna do?"

"Not panic," McBride replied. Although it damn near killed him, he shut down as many emotions as he could and made it into a painful crouch.

Settle, he ordered his mind. Think. The guy couldn't drag Alessandra all over the countryside on foot.

"Did anyone hear a vehicle?"

"No, and I've been listening." Larry's head went up. "People are coming back…"

"Keep them away," McBride told him. "Keep them quiet. What door did he use?"

"Front. He shouted at you not to try and stop him, then…I just don't know. He disappeared."

McBride stood, swayed, found his balance. But it was like running in a nightmare. Every stride forward took forever and seemed to get him nowhere.

At long, long last, however, he reached the motel.

He found his backup on the floor of Ruth's office. Shoving it into the top of his jeans, he checked his Glock, pulled out his cell and speed dialed Larry's number.

"Keep those people back," he said into the phone. Then he ran through the lobby and out into the parking lot.

Two dozen vehicles sat empty under a three-quarter moon. Ruth's faulty sign hummed in the distance. He heard insects and the odd truck far down the road, but in the immediate area, everything remained silent.

He was here, still here, McBride could feel it. Feel Alessandra.

Sensations crawled over him, slithered through him. He recognized the threads of fear and blocked them.

She'd find a way to stall, and he'd want to drag it out in any case. Or at least that was McBride's hope.

The sign made a staticky noise as portions of it winked on and off. Unmoving trees stood to his left and to his right. No one could hide there. Overgrown bushes that stretched half the length of the motel and eventually led to the woods made the most sense. The only sense, really. Assuming once again that insanity ever made sense.

He had to choose, had to do something before he lost Alessandra to a madman.

Fear knotted in his belly. He shoved it down, slammed a lid on it. He loved her. He wouldn't lose her. He wouldn't let her die.

The bushes loomed, dark and misshapen. The sign sizzled and snapped. Frogs and crickets sang. Everything sounded rural and normal.

Everything except the furious, spitting screech that erupted from an obscure spot deep in the distant woods.

"DON'T HURT HIM!"

Alessandra caught the cat Smith hurled into the air with the toe of his boot.

"You stepped on his tail, that's why he screamed."

Smith's breath heaved in and out. "I hate animals."

Alessandra kept a firm hold on Ruth's squirming cat and her eyes on her captor's face. "You brought a dog to the clinic for an examination last Friday."

"I know what I did, and you know why I did it."

He glared at the long scratch Puddles had inflicted on the back of his hand. The hand not holding the knife, Alessandra noted.

"I wanted to kill you that night, leastways that was the plan. Your floozy assistant would leave the clinic, and so would you. No one else around that late. You won't know it, but your car was gonna run out of gas between the clinic and your house. I work with cars and trucks, take 'em apart and put 'em together. You only had a thimbleful of gas in your tank. Enough to start it up for sure, but not much more than that. You getting the picture here, Doc?"

"You tampered with my car, saw to it I'd work late and had a plan for when I ran out of gas."

Did she sound calm, she wondered, or could he hear the panic scrambling inside her?

She released the cat, carefully, and without averting her eyes said, "I understand you want me dead. What I don't understand is why. Who was your wife, and what makes you think I killed her?"

He bared his teeth. "I told you. You changed seats with her. I learned about it after the crash. I talked to people who didn't die. I made sure what was what and who was who. You made her move, and she died because of it. Because of you."

The expression on his face—what Alessandra could see of it in the weak points of light that glowed on the wall behind her—had terror clamoring for release.

He brought the knife back to center between them. "There's four who're responsible. You, who made her move. That lech driver, who kept his brain and his eyesight in his pants. McBride, who got you out before the bus blew, and the bastard brownnoser with the big mouth and excellent driving record, who should have been steering the damn bus in the first place and instead got a promotion for ratting out his slimeball coworker."

"But—"

Penner used the knife to slash the side of the seat. His eyes gleamed. "No buts, lady. My wife's dead, and in a minute, you're gonna be, too."

Memories scattered like ashes in Alessandra's head. The rude woman had started the process. People had moved. Alessandra had moved—from row five to row one. Mother and daughter, seated across from her at that point, were accommodated. Everything was set. Until...

A fragile blonde woman from Arizona who'd been traveling alone had approached her. Why? Because she'd been alone, as well? While the last of the hand luggage was transferred, and with people still milling in the aisle, she'd touched Alessandra's shoulder.

"Excuse me, do you suffer from motion sickness?"

"I said no," Alessandra recalled. Her eyes came up. "Your wife was sitting at the back of the bus. She came to me after most of the seat shuffling was done. She wanted to trade. I didn't ask her to move. She asked me."

"You're lying," Penner growled. "Trying to save your skin. You wanted to be with that man in the back where she'd been sitting. People I talked to said you and him were getting on like nobody's business. Flirting and cooing and having a good old time."

"We were talking, not flirting. He was gay, Penner. He wasn't interested in me."

Penner moved fast, like an angry snake. Except the snake's head stopped an inch from hers.

"Don't matter what he was. You wanted to sit with him, and my Amy made it possible for you to do that."

He was never going to believe her, Alessandra realized with a renewed spurt of fear. It didn't matter what she said, he had his own truth, and he'd kill to avenge it.

For a moment, she thought she spotted a shadow beyond the front windshield.

McBride, or an animal in the bushes?

Swallowing, she prayed she could keep Penner talking.

"Your wife, Amy," she managed to say. "She was very pretty."

Oh, God, it was so lame, but it put a different light in his eyes.

"She was beautiful," he whispered. "Delicate. Like a desert rose." The light deepened to hatred. "That piece-of-scum driver made a pass at her."

His fingers crunched into a ball so tight, Alessandra thought his knuckles might pop through the skin.

"That's why I went for him first. But it didn't work out. Cops figured I was breaking in to steal his money. Moron driver thought so, too. Intruder has a knife and a sack, he must be a thief."

Penner's snarl was a frosty finger skimming along Alessandra's spine.

"So be it, then," he hissed. "I'm caught. I'll go to prison as a thief. When I get out, I'll be more careful. Can't go for the driver straight off, so I'll go for the bitch who I should have gone for in the first place. Her and the man who saved her miserable seat-changing life."

Alessandra struggled not to move, not to do anything that might affect the momentary trance he'd slipped into.

"Got me a dog," he said. "Easy enough to do that. Made sure you stayed late. I even told the floozy I'd be taking a bus from Rapid City to Phoenix, which was the name I gave the dog in case you missed that. I waited out of sight, watched the floozy leave. Perfect. But along came some pissed-off rancher, and I had to wait. Then, damn him to hell, up popped McBride with a bullet in him. I coulda done you both in the parking lot if that rancher hadn't decided to park his truck smack in front of the clinic and have a long talk on his cell phone. He kept eyeballing the door, looked like he was gonna go in and do something to you himself. Then, wouldn't you know it, another rancher pulled up behind him, and they started drinking and cutting up, pulling guns on each other and pretending to shoot."

"I didn't know that," Alessandra admitted in a cautious voice. She stole a glance at the windshield, saw nothing except darkness and felt her stomach muscles cinch. Apparently it hadn't been McBride, after all.

Penner's upper lip curled. "Bang-bang, chug-chug, on and on and on. But finally both ranchers left. I thought, okay, here's my chance. I was moving, already moving, when damned if another SOB didn't muscle in. This one, though, he had the look. I moved on him to get to you—'cause by now I was good and riled and didn't give a rat's ass who died—it wouldn't matter what kind of butt-kicking rifle I had. He'd have shot me first and wouldn't have blinked doing it."

"Eddie," Alessandra said quietly.

A hideous grin split Penner's face. "Was that his name? I never did know. Figured he died, though, because I saw him running, bent and bleeding, that night here at the motel, then I didn't see him again. Fine, I thought to myself, that was him done. It was down to you, me and McBride now."

He used the tip of the blade to draw an X on Alessandra's heart. She pressed her lips together and bit back a reaction.

"So, here we are, Doc, you and me. No McBride for the moment, but he'll come. We're on a bus. Too bad I had to kill the fella who owned it, but he caught me trying to hot-wire the thing, so what else could I do? It's serendipity. You see that, right? You're gonna die the same way my sweet, sweet Amy did, and in a bus, to boot."

An image of the woman she'd crawled past flashed in Alessandra's head, the blonde woman who'd been impaled by a shard of glass from one of the windows.

Something in the trickle of light and shadow outside the bus shifted. As it did, Penner's expression changed. Snapping out a hand, he trapped Alessandra's face and squeezed hard.

"What the hell am I doing?" he demanded in dawning disbelief. "Wasting precious time talking to you? Unless I got lucky and blew him up with that second stick of dynamite, McBride'll be on the hunt. He'll find us, too, he surely will. But when he does, you'll have this knife in your chest and be as dead as my Amy. I'll give him five seconds to look, five more to mourn, then he'll be dead, too. Both of you gone in one night. Hallelujah, justice shall be served."

Alessandra's heart raced as his expression moved from contempt to triumph. His hand shifted to catch her throat and he aimed the knife right at her chest.

Time stopped, she swore it did, but only for a moment. The windshield suddenly smashed apart. When Penner swiveled his head, Alessandra seized the only chance she knew she'd get.

Grabbing his wrist, she knocked his arm with her elbow and aimed a foot at his crotch.

He dodged the kick, but lost his grip on the knife. Like a link in a chain, his hold on her throat also slackened. Not by much, but enough that when she kicked him again, this time in the stomach, she was able to wrench herself free.

She was scrambling for the door when he caught her by the hair and yanked her backward. He swore loud and long, tried to throw her to the floor and pick up his knife at the same time.

All she could see were his legs. Rolling onto her back, she used her foot on his knee.

He let out a howl of pain, then rearing up, bared his teeth and tried to leap over her.

She heard feet landing and glass crunching. Penner cursed louder. There was a thud and an expulsion of air. The next thing she knew, Penner was on the floor, McBride was on top of him and dust and glass were flying in every direction.

"Get out, Alessandra," McBride shouted. He slammed a fist into Penner's face. "Now."

Rage and adrenaline must have fused in Penner, giving him more strength than he might otherwise have possessed. He struck back, got hold of his rifle and batted the gun from McBride's hand.

Alessandra spied the knife in her peripheral vision. She snatched it from the floor. "McBride!"

He caught the hilt when she tossed it to him and deflected the rifle barrel a split second before Penner squeezed off two shots.

"Alessandra, over here!" A frantic Larry beckoned to her through the broken front window. "McBride can take him." As another shot went off, the old man flinched. "I think."

"I can't just leave..." she began, then ducked as yet another shot rang out.

She lifted her head to look and felt her heart stutter in her chest. McBride and Penner had disappeared.

A clunk, a thump and two more shots reached her. From the bushes? She closed her eyes for a brief moment. They'd gone out the emergency exit.

With no idea how to unlock the main door, Alessandra crawled through the broken window and slid down the hood of the bus to the ground.

Larry climbed off the wheel well he'd been balancing on. "Listen," he said as the bushes far ahead of them crackled and snapped. Alessandra would have run toward the sound if a bullet hadn't whizzed past, sending both of them to the ground.

"No, don't!" Larry held her down. "Let McBride do what he's been trained to—"

He was cut off by Penner, who leaped from the underbrush, shoved him aside and launched himself at Alessandra.

She braced. But with very little light and the dense growth making the shadows dark, she didn't actually see what happened next. She only knew she was suddenly lying on her stomach next to Larry, and Penner was no longer there. No more shots rang out, and the sound of fighting simply stopped.

She got back to her knees, squinted into the black. Nothing. There was nothing now except night sounds and Larry breathing heavily behind her.

"McBride?" she whispered.

Still no sound.

Half afraid to move, she called his name again, then let out a scream as a pair of hands gripped her arms from behind.

"It's me." A winded McBride drew her slowly to her feet. "I'm not hurt," he said when she swung to face him. "It's over, darlin'." He reached a hand down to help Larry stand. "He's dead."

"But how?" She swung back. "There were no more shots."

McBride nodded into the darkness. "He fell on the knife. It went right through his chest."

Closing her eyes again, she turned back into him and let his arms encircle her. Relief, regret and exhaustion tumbled through the layer of shock that had seized control of her brain.

McBride was alive. The man who'd tried to kill them was dead. The man whose wife had been impaled by a piece of glass in a bus accident seven years ago had been impaled himself by the very weapon he'd planned to use on the people he'd deemed responsible for his loss. His mistake, together with his obsession, had killed him. What could she or anyone say to that?

As baffled onlookers began to appear, Larry propelled them away.

Alone for the moment McBride tipped Alessandra's head up so he could look into her eyes. "He's gone, we're alive and I'm grateful for both of those things. But I have one big question for you, darlin'. Who the hell was that guy?"

Chapter Eighteen

"I brought you a present, Alessandra." Raven, who'd surprised her by showing up at Moe's rescheduled nine-tieth birthday party, waylaid her near one of the food tables in Larry's barn.

Close to three hundred people had crowded in so far, and Larry predicted another fifty likely would arrive before the night ran out.

"Hasn't been this much excitement in Ben's Creek since the town got its first telephone, and I'm taking my granddad's word on how big that was," he'd confided earlier.

Raven perused the groaning food tables while Alessandra opened the box that had been thrust into her hands.

"Boxing mitts?" She fought a grin, raised a skeptical brow. "I told you on the phone, Raven, I'm not interested in cage boxing."

"Offer stands even so. And they're bag mitts, for practicing. You can use them to fend off creepy men who blame you for their wives' deaths. I got the gory details from a guy with three fingers as I was coming in. Left him trying to figure out how his wife's pooch and my Rip might make a batch of little pit bull puppies."

"Put them in the same room. That should do it."

"Works for me." Raven sampled a bowl of chili. "Man, I wish I could cook like this. So how's McBride, and why isn't he here with you?"

"He and the sheriff are in Lancer. Apparently a death like Penner's creates quadruple the usual paperwork. Add in murder, probable insanity, destruction of private and public property, the list goes on and you've got yourself a supersize headache." She let the grin appear. "On the other hand, McBride's used to all of that, so no big deal, just lots of busywork."

"What about you?"

Alessandra shrugged, sniffed the chili. "I'm good. I'm here, anyway, and unless a certain angry bull breeder or his son-in-law decide I shouldn't be, I'm perfectly safe."

"Are you perfectly happy?"

"Working on it."

"What about plans?"

"I— Hmm. Maybe I want a drink. You?"

"Beer with a whiskey chaser." Raven shrugged at the smile Alessandra sent her. "I'm not a girlie-girl. What can I say? McBride was worried about you, you know, that day he had to take his prisoner down to Cheyenne. I'm talking big-time worried. I think he knew there might be more going on than the fugitive thing. He wanted Clover to watch you, too, but I told him we'd do fine on our own. My opinion? Pretty and polished can be camo for a wildcat. Figure I was right."

"I didn't kill Penner, Raven."

"But you agree he deserved to die."

"I don't know what he deserved. He ran on hate for a very long time. I do think the bull breeder and his son-in-law are lucky to be alive. But then again, so am I."

"Thanks to your husband."

Alessandra dodged the orange-haired woman who'd

been flirting with McBride last night—seriously, only last night?—smiled at Curly over a number of heads and drew Raven to the far barn wall.

"Now that's a bar," the other woman remarked. "Twenty feet of thick plank and acres of bottles behind it. Guess I'll be spending the night in Ben's Creek. How's the infamous local motel for rooms?"

"Most of them need work." Alessandra's eyes sparkled. "Much to the owner's delight. Ruth gets a full reno out of it and won't have to pay a cent."

"He's crazy about you, you know," Raven said. "McBride, I mean, not the dead guy."

Larry walked over, sparing Alessandra the need to respond. "Sheriff's here," he yelled above the newly added sound of a live band. "Means McBride is, too."

"Hey, don't make her run off." Raven pointed at one of the beer kegs and held up two fingers. "I didn't drive all this way just to play Santa Claus and hear a good story. You did a sweet job of fixing me and Rip up after we got hit. I think you should consider opening a clinic in Loden, for people and pets."

"Uh, that's not possible..." Alessandra began, but Larry cut her off, while wagging a finger at Raven.

"Sorry, but we have dibs on that idea. Doc Dyer's about ready to retire. His replacement lives in Lancer and wakes up to his alarm clock playing reveille. Sheriff's getting ready to call it quits, too, so we've got a better than decent job for McBride if he's looking."

"He's not." A pair of familiar arms came down on Alessandra's shoulders. "Was, but he found her, so the looking's done for now. He's also got a departmental leak to expose in Chicago before he does anything that involves change... With one beautiful exception."

"I think that's our cue to scram, Larry." Raven picked

up the beer she'd ordered, handed the second one to him. "Fifty bucks says I can take the toughest female—or man under one-eighty—in an arm-wrestling match."

"You really do have to love small towns," Alessandra remarked in their wake. She swung on her heel to smile at McBride. "So." Her arms hooked loosely around his neck. "Here we are—you, me and a bunch of people we didn't even know existed last week at this time."

"Is that good or bad?"

"It's, well…you, really. Your life, your world. Danger's an integral part of your makeup, McBride. You wouldn't be complete without it hovering around you like a vulture."

"I'd rather see it as circling me like a hawk, but go on."

"You wouldn't be complete," she repeated, "and wouldn't be the man I fell in love with seven years ago." She ran her fingers over the bullet wound healing beneath his shirt. "I'll admit, I'm not as driven as you are to live and work on that fine line between life and death, but I think I see the difference now between living on the edge and having a death wish."

"I don't have a death wish, darlin'." His eyes glittered. "At least, I haven't for the past seven years."

"Penner used the word *serendipity* a lot while he was holding me on that bus."

"I'm not sure I want to think about that right now."

"Neither do I," she agreed. "But the serendipity part, the concept of a happy accident, does fit. It applies. To us. To how we met. I'm being metaphorical, because the actual bus crash was a horrible accident and people died, but us accidentally meeting that night was a good thing, the best thing that's ever happened to me."

"And me."

"There you go, then." She bumped him with her hips. "I want to adopt a dog."

"What?"

"A German shepherd with a white arrow on his back."

McBride stared at her. "You want to adopt Penner's dog."

"He wasn't Penner's dog, he was Penner's patsy. I want to call him Rio, because after you've exposed the leak in your department, I think we should take a vacation."

"We, as in you and me?"

"Joan'll dog sit."

"While we're in Rio. Together."

She fingered the delicate chain that held her wedding rings. "We are still married, McBride. We'll see where these—and yours—end up when we get back."

"From Rio."

"My mother loved it there. Pretty sure you told me you loved it there, too." Moving all the way in, she shimmied her lower body temptingly against his. "Choice is yours. I can always go alone."

"Don't think so, darlin'." He pulled her hips against his. "Give me a week, two tops, and we're on that plane."

"Well, then." Kissing him slowly on the mouth, she twined her fingers in his hair, then let her eyes sparkle into his. "I'm half-afraid to say it, but I really do love you, Marshal McBride. I don't love all the secrets you keep, but you're improving there. I also don't love every aspect of your work, but it occurs to me that you wouldn't like euthanizing someone's pet, either. Not that I enjoy euthanizing any living creature, but you know what I mean. Everything's relative, in love and work."

A smile appeared on his face, lighting his eyes. "That was a pretty convoluted statement, but the fact of it is, I love you right back. A lot. Even if you did kill some of the romance with the pet thing."

"You think?" The tease inside her smile blossomed. With her fingers still curled in his hair, she pulled his head down until his mouth was less than an inch from hers. "In that case, what say we forget about work altogether and give our full attention to the romance side of things? Let serendipity take over and see where we wind up."

"Long as we wind up there together," McBride agreed.

And covering her mouth with his, he took her on a ride more wild than the one that had brought them together seven years ago.

* * * * *

INTRIGUE

COMING NEXT MONTH

Available September 13, 2011

#1299 THE BLACK SHEEP SHEIK
Cowboys Royale
Dana Marton

#1300 DETECTIVE DADDY
Situation: Christmas
Mallory Kane

#1301 SCENE OF THE CRIME: WIDOW CREEK
Carla Cassidy

#1302 PHANTOM OF THE FRENCH QUARTER
Shivers: Vieux Carré Captives
Colleen Thompson

#1303 THE BIG GUNS
Mystery Men
HelenKay Dimon

#1304 WESTIN'S WYOMING
Open Sky Ranch
Alice Sharpe

You can find more information on upcoming
Harlequin® titles, free excerpts and more at
www.HarlequinInsideRomance.com.

HICNM0811

REQUEST YOUR FREE BOOKS!
2 FREE NOVELS PLUS 2 FREE GIFTS!

Harlequin

INTRIGUE

BREATHTAKING ROMANTIC SUSPENSE

YES! Please send me 2 FREE Harlequin Intrigue® novels and my 2 FREE gifts (gifts are worth about \$10). After receiving them, if I don't wish to receive any more books, I can return the shipping statement marked "cancel." If I don't cancel, I will receive 6 brand-new novels every month and be billed just \$4.49 per book in the U.S. or \$5.24 per book in Canada. That's a saving of at least 14% off the cover price! It's quite a bargain! Shipping and handling is just 50¢ per book in the U.S. and 75¢ per book in Canada.* I understand that accepting the 2 free books and gifts places me under no obligation to buy anything. I can always return a shipment and cancel at any time. Even if I never buy another book, the two free books and gifts are mine to keep forever.

182/382 HDN FEQ2

Name	(PLEASE PRINT)
Address	Apt. #
City	State/Prov.	Zip/Postal Code

Signature (if under 18, a parent or guardian must sign)

Mail to the **Reader Service:**
IN U.S.A.: P.O. Box 1867, Buffalo, NY 14240-1867
IN CANADA: P.O. Box 609, Fort Erie, Ontario L2A 5X3
Not valid for current subscribers to Harlequin Intrigue books.

**Are you a subscriber to Harlequin Intrigue books
and want to receive the larger-print edition?
Call 1-800-873-8635 or visit www.ReaderService.com.**

* Terms and prices subject to change without notice. Prices do not include applicable taxes. Sales tax applicable in N.Y. Canadian residents will be charged applicable taxes. Offer not valid in Quebec. This offer is limited to one order per household. All orders subject to credit approval. Credit or debit balances in a customer's account(s) may be offset by any other outstanding balance owed by or to the customer. Please allow 4 to 6 weeks for delivery. Offer available while quantities last.

Your Privacy—The Reader Service is committed to protecting your privacy. Our Privacy Policy is available online at www.ReaderService.com or upon request from the Reader Service.

We make a portion of our mailing list available to reputable third parties that offer products we believe may interest you. If you prefer that we not exchange your name with third parties, or if you wish to clarify or modify your communication preferences, please visit us at www.ReaderService.com/consumerschoice or write to us at Reader Service Preference Service, P.O. Box 9062, Buffalo, NY 14269. Include your complete name and address.

HI11B

New York Times *and* USA TODAY *bestselling author*
Maya Banks presents a brand-new miniseries

PREGNANCY & PASSION

When four irresistible tycoons face
the consequences of temptation.

Book 1—ENTICED BY HIS FORGOTTEN LOVER

Available September 2011 from Harlequin® Desire®!

Rafael de Luca had been in bad situations before. A crowded ballroom could never make him sweat.

These people would never know that he had no memory of any of them.

He surveyed the party with grim tolerance, searching for the source of his unease.

At first his gaze flickered past her, but he yanked his attention back to a woman across the room. Her stare bored holes through him. Unflinching and steady, even when his eyes locked with hers.

Petite, even in heels, she had a creamy olive complexion. A wealth of inky-black curls cascaded over her shoulders and her eyes were equally dark.

She looked at him as if she'd already judged him and found him lacking. He'd never seen her before in his life. Or had he?

He cursed the gaping hole in his memory. He'd been diagnosed with selective amnesia after his accident four months ago. Which seemed like complete and utter bull. No one got amnesia except hysterical women in bad soap operas.

With a smile, he disengaged himself from the group

around him and made his way to the mystery woman.

She wasn't coy. She stared straight at him as he approached, her chin thrust upward in defiance.

"Excuse me, but have we met?" he asked in his smoothest voice.

His gaze moved over the generous swell of her breasts pushed up by the empire waist of her black cocktail dress.

When he glanced back up at her face, he saw fury in her eyes.

"Have we *met?*" Her voice was barely a whisper, but he felt each word like the crack of a whip.

Before he could process her response, she nailed him with a right hook. He stumbled back, holding his nose.

One of his guards stepped between Rafe and the woman, accidentally sending her to one knee. Her hand flew to the folds of her dress.

It was then, as she cupped her belly, that the realization hit him. She was pregnant.

Her eyes flashing, she turned and ran down the marble hallway.

Rafael ran after her. He burst from the hotel lobby, and saw two shoes sparkling in the moonlight, twinkling at him.

He blew out his breath in frustration and then shoved the pair of sparkly, ultrafeminine heels at his head of security.

"Find the woman who wore these shoes."

Will Rafael find his mystery woman?
Find out in Maya Banks's passionate new novel
ENTICED BY HIS FORGOTTEN LOVER
Available September 2011 from Harlequin® Desire®!